CULT

A NOVEL

J.L. POND

For Tiffany,
who believed in me,
always,
even and especially when she
had no reason to

PREFACE

I thought I had faith.

My earliest memories are filled with stories from the Bible, and they've always made sense to me. Adam and Eve and David and Goliath and Peter and Paul always seemed as real to me as Ben Franklin or Amelia Earhart or any of a thousand other historical figures. The stories of God's interactions with humanity always rang with an air of reality as strong as any of the battles at Bastogne and Bunker Hill.

Believing in God and the Bible seemed the easiest thing in the world. But as high school's final year dawned, something had changed, and I found I wasn't at all prepared for it.

But I'm getting ahead of myself. Let's start at the beginning…

1

My name is Nathan Rudolph, and my friends call me Rudy. Ask anyone you like, and they'd tell you that Rudy Rudolph is an ideal Christian teenager. I've always been respectful, well-spoken, known more about the Bible than most, and played piano for worship.

Church should have worked for me, and I guess it did for a long time.

I can't tell you when "it" started. It's like getting sick. By the time you actually notice that you don't feel well, your body's already been sending you signals for a while. You just weren't paying attention.

Maybe it started last semester. We had a debate class in school, and I had to defend creationism against evolution. *Great,* I thought, *this'll be easy!* Everyone knew the evolution-ists didn't have a leg to stand on. I'd have an easy A.

No dice. My opponent was not only way better prepared for the debate, but she made some good points that I'd never thought about before. I think that was the first time I *really* wondered if what I believed about God was as sound as I'd been told.

Or maybe it started in ninth grade. A friend's father committed suicide, and as far as I was told it came right out of the blue. The family, of course, was devastated. They'd been going to our church for years, and I remember hearing my parents talk about whether or not Christians go to heaven if they kill themselves. I don't remember them ever coming to an answer, and everyone else did their level best to avoid the topic.

But who knows? Maybe this whole thing began when I was twelve. Mom and Dad hit a rough patch that culminated in Dad having an affair. I don't know how long it went on before he broke it off and confessed the whole thing. I've never seen Mom cry like she did during that period. I went to bed every night for a month terrified of what the dawn would bring. For the first time in my life I was forced to question things about our family that previously seemed unquestionable. Could Mom and Dad split up? What would happen? Would my brother and I be separated? Would Zach and I each have to pick a parent? I had friends that had been through that, and it sounded miserable.

After a long and painful few months, life slowly returned to normal. But my faith in the reliability of family was shaken.

Like I said, I can't say for sure when the doubting began, but by the end of my sophomore year in high school, I wasn't sure what I believed anymore. Dad had always said that I could come to him with any questions I had, but it wasn't easy. How do you admit to your own father that you have doubts about your faith, particularly when he's already proven incapable of living up to his own? To make matters worse, he'd always had a short temper, and more than one encounter had taught me to be wary of challenging him.

So, what do you do with doubt when you're a sixteen-year-old conservative Christian surrounded by other conservative Christians?

You bury it, of course.

Pastor B's office is at the back of the sanctuary at Riverside Christian, through a door behind the stage suggesting the church's architect moonlighted designing courthouses. Opening the door, I felt like I was walking into the judge's chambers.

"Good morning, Nathan! How are you this morning?" Pastor B asked with more energy than it seemed right for anyone to have this early on a Friday. He wasn't young, but he'd always been rather spry for a man of his years.

"Oh, I'm fine," I said, walking that thin line between the truth and the lie. Physically, I *was* fine. Spiritually? Emotionally? Well, he didn't specify the parameters of the question now, did he?

"Glad to hear it! Come on in and make yourself comfortable." He gestured toward a set of couches set opposite each other in the middle of the room. "Can I get you some coffee?"

I shrugged. "You have any creamer?"

"Sure do! Drink it black myself, but I find most folks like

some kinda flavorin'. French vanilla or hazelnut?"

"Hazelnut, please. Two parts coffee to one part creamer."

Pastor B laughed. "That's a lot of sugar."

"It's an early Friday, Pastor."

"Fair enough." He fixed the coffee and brought it over.

He sat down across from me as I took a swig. The sweetness was almost sickening, but I wanted the caffeine and couldn't drink the stuff any other way.

"So, Nathan, tell me. What can I do for you?"

I took another sip of the 66.6% coffee, stalling. I wondered for a moment if Satan would take his coffee the same way, just for the symbolism.

"Well, Pastor. I, uh... I guess I wanted to talk about Sunday. I mean your message, from last week."

So, it's like this. Last year, some of the guys at school got smartphones and the accompanying unfettered access to the internet. Their parents must have had some kind of next-level naiveté to think A) that the guys weren't totally full of crap with all of their "reasons" for why they needed smartphones in the first place, B) that teenage boys would never use smartphones for porn, and C) that they would be able to do any kind of meaningful monitoring of the web activity on such devices.

I'd seen *things* before then. I'd seen the lingerie models in Mom's department store catalogues. I'd run into uninvited pop-ups when researching a school paper or something like that. Mostly I'd just close them and move on, but there'd been times that Mom and Dad had been out, and I'd clicked instead of closing.

Those browser histories are so easy to clear.

I'd been doing that kind of thing in private for a couple years, but with the guys now carrying their own personal web portals…let's just say things escalated. At first, everyone tried to pretend that they had never done and would never do anything like that, but the lies were quickly abandoned. We all knew everyone else was full of it. So, what the heck?

Sure, it felt wrong at first. But the more time went by, the more it just didn't. Until one Sunday morning in August. Pastor Bennington was talking about the Sermon on the Mount when he came to this little gem in Matthew: "But I tell you that anyone who looks at a woman lustfully has already committed adultery with her in his heart." Pastor B said it was just as wrong to want to have sex with a woman you weren't married to as it was to actually have sex with her.

At the time, I wasn't sure I bought it. Surely Mom would have preferred if Dad had just looked instead of actually sleeping with another woman. Common sense seemed to say there was a difference there.

But despite my attempt to blow him off, Pastor B's sermon rattled around my head throughout the next week. If the lusting counted as adultery, then how did that play into all of the verses that said that adulterers wouldn't inherit the Kingdom of God? What *exactly* did it mean?

My buried doubt was pushing its way through the dirt, like some undead terror. I tried to forget about the sermon, but it kept nagging at me. I'd prayed the Sinner's Prayer when I was five and had been operating under the assumption that I was saved ever since. But how could I be saved and yet in danger of not inheriting the Kingdom? Could it mean I wasn't saved?

The questions piled on.

I didn't want to talk to Mom or Dad about it, for obvious reasons. I didn't really want to talk to the pastor about it either, but the questions wouldn't go away. They demanded to be answered, and as hard as I tried to ignore it, I knew if Pastor B was right those answers could affect eternity.

Cut to Friday morning.

"Ah, the Sermon on the Mount," Pastor B said, nodding.

"Yeah. Well, not the Sermon itself, I guess. But one verse in particular. It said something about looking at women being the same as adultery."

I paused here, and Pastor B nodded. "Yep, that's a hard one for a lot of folks to wrap their heads around."

"Does it really mean that?" I asked. "I mean, well... I don't know. I guess, maybe it just seems like..." I trailed off. This was feeling a bit more uncomfortable than I'd anticipated, and I didn't really want to get to the chase.

Pastor B seemed to know what I was thinking. "Let me guess. Not the easiest thing *not* looking these days, is it?"

I shrugged. "Not really."

He nodded. "I hear you. Seems the more years go by the tighter and smaller most ladies' clothing gets. But I'm guessin' that's probably not all you're talkin' about, is it?

I looked at my coffee. Couldn't even manage an acknowledgement, but I figured my silence would provide all the answer he needed.

"Hmm," he said, nodding. "All too common these days, Nathan. Impossible to avoid, really. Whether at home, school, a friend's house…seems like every man has to deal with pornography at one time in his life or another. Anymore, it almost always starts in adolescence. Most men deal with it throughout their entire lives."

That caught me off guard. I'd expected him to rail against the evils of lust and condemn me for being such a perv. I thought about the men in the church and wondered who Pastor B meant when he said "most men."

"But, what do the other verses mean then?" I asked.

"Which other verses?"

"I looked them up after your sermon on Sunday." I pulled the Bible off the table sitting between us. It took a minute to find the right page. "Here it is. First Corinthians 6. Verses nine and ten seem to say that adulterers will not inherit the kingdom of God. And you said that it was pretty much the same thing to look at a woman with lust as it was to sleep with her. It sounds like it's basically saying that if someone lusts, they won't be saved."

Pastor B nodded slowly. A small, sympathetic, vaguely superior smile played at the corners of his mouth. "I think I see your problem."

My "problem?" Okay…

"This passage isn't talkin' about Christians," he continued. "It's talkin' about unbelievers, people who never repent of their sin. You believe that Jesus died and rose again right?"

I nodded.

"And you've prayed the Sinner's Prayer, right? You've told God you're sorry for what you've done and asked him to forgive you?"

More nodding.

"Then that's it. Christ's finished work on the cross means that we are forgiven of all of our sins, past, present, and future."

I frowned. "But, you just said most men deal with this... well, forever. What happens if I can't stop?"

He offered that superior smile again. "Nathan, God knows the challenges you face as a young man in this time. The Bible says that Jesus understands because he was tempted in every way like we are. You should certainly try to not look at porn. But if you fail, just trust him and repent. He'll forgive you *every* time. He'll always want you to come back to him."

"It seems too easy."

"That's the beauty of grace. It definitely wasn't easy for Christ, but it can be for us. We just have to humble ourselves and keep coming back to him. All he expects of us is our faith in him. He takes care of the rest."

I couldn't really think of anything else to say, and a few moments of silence went by before Pastor B asked, "Can I pray for you, Nathan?"

I actually kinda hated it when people prayed for me. It didn't happen too often, but when it did I always felt weird and self-conscious. But how do you tell your pastor you *don't* want him to pray for you?

"Sure, that'd be great."

He came around and sat on the couch next to me, a bit too close for me to feel comfortable, and put a hand on my shoulder. "Almighty Father," he began. "I come before you this mornin' to pray for my brother, Nathan. I see such a desire in him to please you, Father, and to live a right life before you. I pray that you will strengthen him through this battle, and convince him beyond all doubt of your love for him. Whenever he fails to measure up to your standard, Lord, I pray your love would draw him back to you, and that he would find at your feet all the grace he needs to carry on. We thank you, Father, for your forgiveness and your love. In Jesus' holy name, Amen."

He opened his eyes and took his hand off my shoulder.

"Thanks, Pastor," I said, standing to leave. "I appreciate you taking the time to listen."

"Anytime at all, Nathan. That's what I'm here for."

2

The following Monday marked the start of my senior year. Every year I held out hope that they wouldn't start school on a Monday. Make it a Thursday or something, and ease us back in with a short week.

But every August, life kicked me in the teeth again, and I rolled out of bed way too early on a Monday morning.

Knight's Day Academy is a private Christian school, so there's no bus service. Dad teaches history at Longview Community College, and Knight's Day is just off his route to work. So, most days he was my ride to and from school. That morning, however, Simon was coming by in his used-but-new-to-him Toyota Corolla. The thing looked like it had about a half million miles on it, but it still ran. It was almost embarrassing to be seen getting in and out of the thing, but when you're seventeen any car means freedom.

Sim and I had been best friends since kindergarten. His family moved to Denver following his dad's retirement from the Army. He'd done something with electronics and now worked for the local HP plant. Their house was substantially larger than ours, and Sim's parents could easily have afforded to buy him a nicer car than the ancient Corolla. But his folks, like mine, made every effort to ensure he wasn't spoiled or entitled. He complained about it at first, but stopped when I pointed out that he at least owned his car. I turned seventeen in March, and my parents' birthday gift was a key to our 1997 Ford Taurus station wagon. They made it crystal clear that, "The car's not yours, but it's yours to use."

Sim and I decided a couple weeks before the term that it'd be marginally less embarrassing to be seen exiting an ancient sedan than an ancient station wagon. So, I'd chip in a little gas money, and he'd handle the driving.

I stumbled into the dining room about twenty minutes before Sim was scheduled to show up. My hair was "sort of" brushed in a way that said, "You can make me try, but you can't make me try that hard." Mom was in the kitchen.

"Good morning!"

"Morning," was all I managed back. School was starting, *and* it was a Monday. Not sure the morning qualified as "good."

"Simon's picking you up, right?"

"Yup. He'll drop me off after school."

"Great! Should make things a little simpler this year with you boys being able to get yourselves around."

I nodded, trying to look happier than I felt. Mom has always been one of those people that puts a high premium on pleasantness. If you can't actually be happy, at least try to fake it.

I poured a bowl of Cap'n Crunch, and watched the clock tick down the last precious minutes of my summer. Sim pulled into the drive five minutes early and honked twice. I dumped the mostly empty bowl in the sink, hugged Mom, and left.

Someone once said that the more things change, the more they stay the same. I'm pretty sure the author of that quote was in high school when they came up with it.

Senior year. After a morning of introductory class periods, it was clear this would be an awful lot like junior year, though perhaps a bit harder. Sim and I had Algebra II together for first period. Seemed like a good idea. Get math out of the way early. But no one should have to sit through Algebra at 8:00 a.m. If there's not a provision to that effect in the Geneva Convention, there really should be.

Then our schedules diverged. I had American Lit for second period, free period for third, then lunch. We met back in the cafeteria with prepackaged sack lunches. From the look on his face as he walked up to the corner table I'd claimed, it was clear Sim was feeling every bit as moody as I was. But while I tend to brood in silence, Sim is burdened by no such restraint.

"That's it, dude. I can't take it anymore. I'm calling P.T. Heck with this nonsense."

Sim has been threatening to drop out and run off to join Barnum and Bailey since seventh grade. We all have our coping mechanisms.

"Rough morning?" I asked.

"It's absurd!" he said, running his hand through his curly red hair. "You were there for the cruel and unusual punishment that was Algebra II. Thank goodness for the nap during free period, because third was Spanish II. Why do my parents insist on this? Do they not understand that with the progress of voice-to-text and translation softwares the language barrier will be non-existent by the time I get out of college?"

For all of his excellent best-friend qualities, Sim did have the annoying habit of talking about tech and other geek-ridden topics that no one else cared about.

"Couldn't talk 'em out of it?"

He shook his head. "I tried, man. All last month. I even wrote a freaking report outlining all of the progresses in automated translation. Then I used Google Translate to render the whole thing in Spanish."

I raised an eyebrow, impressed. "Wow. They still wouldn't bite?"

Sim rolled his eyes. "Nope. Dad took it to work and had some guy who grew up in Mexico read it. He then took red ink and circled every place the language wasn't grammatically perfect. He said, 'When Google Translate actually learns Spanish, you can use it. Until then, you're taking Spanish II'."

I laughed, and he glared at me. "Sorry, dude," I said. "But that's totally your dad."

He sighed. "I know. I should have expected it. The man's a freaking drill sergeant sometimes."

A passing teacher cleared her throat at Sim's use of the

faux-F-word. But, he *technically* hadn't said anything offensive, so they couldn't *technically* do anything about it. The whole school had been getting away with such "cursing" for as long as anyone could remember. It was pitiful, but discipline at Knight's Day borders on the draconian, so we rebel in whatever small ways won't get us expelled.

Sim opened his sack lunch and removed a ham sandwich. Taking a bite, he said, "So, what about you? How was AmLit?"

I shrugged. "About what you'd expect. We'll be reading a bunch of books written by people long dead that someone decided are still worth reading. *The Great Gatsby* and *The Crucible* are both in the syllabus for this semester. Next term we get into Brit-lit."

"Guess I'll have that to look forward to tomorrow. This new format is gonna take some getting used to."

I nodded. Knight's Day was introducing a collegiate style format to get us ready for what we'd face in most universities. We'd have MWF classes and TR classes. The worst part as far as we were concerned was that the new schedule meant every class on Tuesdays and Thursdays would be 50% longer than it ever was before. I'd have an hour and a half of Church History, Biology, and Intro to Accounting.

I made a mental note to put some Advil in my backpack when I got home.

Sim finished his sandwich in relative silence, then reached in his backpack and pulled out an Algebra textbook.

I groaned. "Dude, we've got twenty minutes left before

the bell rings. You really want to dive into homework already?"

He shook his head, smiling. "Not homework." He opened the book to the back cover and lifted the inside dust jacket. Taped beneath was a microSD card.

"What's that?" I asked.

"Way more fun than homework," he said. "I found this stuff last night. You gotta check it out."

I hesitated, Friday's conversation with Pastor B playing over in my head.

"I don't know, man. I don't even think I could. There's no way my computer has a slot for this."

"I know, but I gotcha covered." He unzipped a small pocket on his backpack and dug around for a second before retrieving what appeared to be a standard SD card. "It's an adapter. I know your computer has an SD card slot. You just insert the microSD card into the adapter here, and you're set."

I took the cards from him and stared at them for a moment. Finally, I said, "I don't know, Sim. What if my parents catch me with this?"

Sim laughed. "Seriously? What makes you think your folks would have the first clue what this was even if they did find it?"

"What if they ask?"

"Then lie!" he said, a bit louder than I'd have preferred. He seemed to realize it, too, because when he continued, his voice was lower. "Just tell them it's a new way the classes are disseminating homework assignments. Paper reduction or something. You really think they're going to press you?"

I knew he was right. My parents weren't stupid, but they definitely weren't the most tech savvy folks. Still, Pastor B's voice was echoing in my head. *"You should certainly try…"*

"Just don't take the files off the chip," Sim pressed. "If your parents stumble in your room or something, eject it. There won't be a shred of evidence left on that antiquated machine you call a laptop."

I tried in vain to come up with some excuse, but the truth was my curiosity had kicked in, and I wanted to know what he'd found. Finally, I slipped the cards into my wallet.

"Let me know what you think," Sim said with a grin.

I flashed my own grin, one I didn't feel. But hey, I hadn't done anything wrong. It was just an SD card. The Bible didn't say anything about not having an SD card in one's wallet, did it?

I'd feared that dinner would be a painful affair. Don't get me wrong, dinners with my family were normally pretty okay. My parents genuinely cared about each other, and Zach, my fifteen-year-old brother, had gotten far less annoying in the last couple years. Another year or two and we might even be friends.

But the end of the first day of any term meant an onslaught of questions about new classes and old friends and new teachers, and on, and on. Mom and Dad wanted me to be happy and excited about school, so I feigned happiness and excitement. It's an old game, and one I'd gotten pretty good at by this point. Smile, and throw a little energy behind the opening sentence. Then make each anecdote interesting, but not too interesting. It's important that there be nothing too compelling in each story, or else they'd ask more questions.

I must have done well because the attention soon shifted to Zach, then to Mom and Dad's respective work days. Soon enough, dinner was eaten and the dishes were cleaned.

I retreated to my room to get started on the obligatory homework that teachers always insist on assigning on the first day. Second term of my freshman year, Mr. Harbaugh announced that he would be assigning no homework that day as a treat to welcome us to the new term. We loved him for it, but it's ruined me. Every term since, I've held out hope that my teachers would be as merciful, and every term that hope was dashed to pieces on the rocks of knowledge assessments and remedial worksheets. "To prep us for new material," they said.

To destroy joy and blot out all light from the world was more like it.

I worked through half a sheet of Algebra problems, pleasantly surprised at how much my brain seemed to have retained over the summer. I could hear the sound of Zach's Xbox One reverberating through the wall, and the muted dialogue coming from the movie my folks were watching in the living room. Some romantic comedy, I think. Everyone had more or less settled in for the night, and the house was getting quiet.

Since dinner ended, I'd been trying to ignore the SD cards tucked into the wallet I'd left on the dresser. But in the relative quiet of the rest of the house, they might as well have been screaming at me from across the room.

I got up and moved to pick up the wallet. I slid out the cards, amazed again at how small they were. The technology wasn't new, but it still impressed me that they could fit so much data on something so small. The card Sim had given me had a storage capacity of 16 GB. I wondered if he'd actually filled the thing, or if it was just the one he'd had in his phone at the time.

Moving back to the desk, I sat down and stared at the cards. As innocuous as they looked lying there next to the computer, it was hard to believe what they actually held.

I fought with myself. My curiosity was at a slow but steady burn, a strange excitement welling in my chest. I remembered what Pastor B had said, and I tried to fight it. I tried to convince myself that it was wrong, that I shouldn't do this.

But the cards weren't going away. They sat on the desk, unchanging. Inevitable.

I went into the kitchen under the guise of getting a glass of water. Mom was leaning into Dad, his arm wrapped around her as the movie played on. I checked the timer on the player. Half an hour in. Should be at least an hour till the end then. And Zach would be busy with his game until Dad knocked on his door and told him to go to bed.

Returning to my room, I closed the door and moved my computer and algebra work to the bed, positioning every-thing so the screen wouldn't be visible from the door. I laid out the Algebra book, put a pencil between my teeth, and plugged in some headphones. I opened my web browser and ran a "how-to" search for the next problem on the worksheet, just in case Dad happened to come in and ask what I was working on. I also opened iTunes and set the player on pause in the middle of a song in the middle of an album.

Dad had only ever done a spot check on my computer activity once or twice, but the last thing I wanted was for him to walk in during whatever Sim had loaded on this card.

Everything in place, I grabbed the cards from the desk, slipped the microSD card into its adaptor, and sat back on the bed. For another moment, I wrestled with whether or not I should.

But like I said. Inevitable.

3

The rest of the week continued pretty much like that. Wake up, breakfast, classes, lunch with Sim, dinner, homework. Sim had new SD cards almost daily. He'd long collected old electronics that his dad brought home from the office, and his supply of cards seemed almost limitless, as did his access to new and exotic content with which to fill them.

I felt guilty, but Sim was right. My folks had no interest in what I did on my own time. School nights were for homework. As long as my report cards remained favorable, they were happy to assume that I was doing exactly what I was supposed to be doing in my room on a school night.

But you know what they say about assumptions.

Every night proceeded the same way. I'd nearly finish my homework, then set up as though I was scanning the Internet for the answer to some question just in case they knocked on my door. Then, SD cards.

I tried. Honestly, I really tried. Pastor B said I should, and I did. But the pull of this thing was like nothing else in the world. It felt like I was wired for it.

As I laid in bed each night trying to fall asleep, it felt as though the weight of heaven itself bore down on my soul. The excitement I'd felt before plugging in the SD cards was replaced with an almost crushing guilt. Every time I'd pray for God to forgive me, to help me do better. I'd swear before sleep claimed me that I wouldn't take the new SD card from Sim at lunch, and that I'd give back all the ones I already had.

But I couldn't do it. Lunch would come, and the curiosity would return. Dinner. Homework. SD card. Guilt. Repentance.

Rinse. Repeat.

By Friday, the amount of repentance required to feel even remotely right with God was getting tiresome. Pastor B had said God would forgive me, but I didn't feel very forgiven. I felt trapped. Imprisoned.

Lost.

I woke up Saturday morning to a day that reflected my mood. Thick clouds covered the sky giving everything a heavy, gray feeling.

For the past few years, my Saturdays have not been my own. At Pastor B's urging, and my parents' "encouragement," I'd been playing the piano during Sunday morning worship. From the beginning, I wasn't keen on the idea. Perhaps that's because it would require playing in front of the whole church on a regular basis. Maybe I just didn't want to be responsible for wrecking the worship mood if I made some noticeable mistake.

But truth be told, I think the biggest reason I didn't want

to do it is that the worship team practices at 9 a.m. every Saturday.

Saturday morning. The one time that should be a sacred, untouchable haven of teenage rest, and I'd been spending it playing the piano for going on four years now.

So, there I was, still rocking the previous night's guilt like some twisted emotional hangover, the day looking as bleak as my heart felt, and I was going to spend the morning playing praise and worship music.

Add hypocrisy to the list of things feeding my guilt.

I rolled out of bed at 8:15, and pulled on a shirt and jeans that were only semi-wrinkled. Pastor B tended to frown on hats in church, but I guess he'd decided against getting touchy with the church's premier pianist on a Saturday morning.

I half-walked, half-stumbled into the sanctuary at 8:55. The guitarists and bassist were already on stage getting set up. I noticed that the drummer hadn't arrived yet.

Gary Messner led our worship team. He smiled at me as I trudged up the steps to the piano.

"Late night?" he asked.

If you only knew. "Yeah," I replied. "I really should know better by now."

Gary laughed. "Don't sweat it. You're supposed to be sleep deprived at your age. We won't get into anything too rough this morning."

I nodded, but didn't say anything. The advantage to specializing in jazz piano is that the style of music we performed in church was child's play. He could pull the most difficult songs out of our repertoire, and they still wouldn't count as "rough".

Gary handed me the list of songs we'd be running. He wasn't kidding. I could work through the list in my sleep. For a moment, I strongly considered attempting that very thing.

Five minutes past our scheduled start time, David Kyle walked in the sanctuary's main door. Actually, walked might be the wrong word. He almost fell through the door. As he struggled up the steps to the stage, Gary raised an eyebrow. "My, my. Rough nights must be contagious."

David grunted, but it sounded more like a groan. He obviously hadn't showered, and if I were to venture a guess, I'd say he must have worn the same clothes on Friday.

Everyone kept watching him. "Seriously, David. What happened?" Gary asked.

David was busy fishing out a pair of ear plugs. I had noticed there were days that he used them and days that he didn't, but I had yet to discern any kind of pattern.

"One too many. Let's just get a move on, eh?" David said.

Gary laughed, as though this were a picture of normalcy. "Guess Rudy's not the only one in for a rough morning." The other guitarist and bassist laughed, too, as though the whole scene was comedic gold.

I forced an amused smile, but I was thinking back to my meeting with Pastor B. Adulterers weren't the only ones who wouldn't inherit the Kingdom of God. Drunkards were on the list, too.

I tried to shove the thought away as Gary started the first song on the list, but I'd been right. I could play through this list in my sleep, and my mind drifted back to the question.

Was drunkenness another thing like lust or adultery? Was whether or not we were sorry for it after the fact all that mattered to God?

I started to question Pastor B's explanation. If he was right, then David could get drunk every night, I could watch porn every night, heck someone could commit murder every night. All that would matter as far as God was concerned was whether or not we repented afterwards. Something in that didn't feel right.

It just seemed way too easy.

None of the events of Saturday morning proved enough to keep me from visiting the SD cards again on Saturday night. In fact, with Mom and Dad out on a date and Zach spending the night at a friend's house, it was easier than ever to yield to their siren call.

As I lay in bed wrestling with the emotional aftermath, I waffled between two warring emotions. On one hand, I was almost relieved. If David could be a drunkard and a Christian, one that even plays in a church worship band and occasionally teaches Sunday school, then maybe it was okay that I had my problems with lust. Maybe God really did understand how hard it was being a human in this world. Maybe he really did love us in spite of the mess and just wanted us to feel sorry and come back to him afterwards.

I tried to believe that. But every time I tried to let relief well up, guilt reared its head and beat the relief senseless. Hours after I'd gone to bed, I finally fell asleep. But it was fitful, and I woke Sunday morning feeling just as tired as when I'd gone to bed.

I arrived at church forty-five minutes before Sunday school. The worship team always showed up early to give the praise program one last run-through. I noticed David looked a bit rough again, though he covered for it better than he had the previous morning. He reached for the ear plugs, and I knew that he'd been drinking again. Probably heavily.

I wondered, did David spend his nights like I did? Did he wrestle with God, seeking repentance for failing yet again to live up to the standard?

David's apparent hangover notwithstanding, praise prep went smoothly and everyone split into various Sunday school groups. The youth group had been working through Leviticus. Yeah, Leviticus. But at least there were donuts. And 66.6% coffee.

After Sunday school let out, I headed for the sanctuary to do one last check, making sure everything was in order. It'd been years since I'd messed something up badly enough to be noticeable during worship, but that didn't warrant getting sloppy.

Pastor B opened the service welcoming everyone, and a special welcome to our visitors, and we're thrilled you're with us, and yada, yada, yada. I wondered if he ever bothered to check whether we actually had any visitors, or if he figured it'd be a morale boost for folks to think that the outside world cared enough to send some.

Gary took over giving the requisite invitation for everyone to stand. Given the lack of challenge presented by the week's music, my mind was left free to wonder if God cared whether anyone stood when Gary told them to. Sure, he might care if people actually wanted to stand, but if everyone preferred to stay seated, did it mean anything that they stood at Gary's urging?

We played a few songs, and people sang. A few people raised their hands. I'd noticed from my perch on the stage that it was always the same three people. No one else would be caught dead making such a display.

Then the offering and communion. I played a mildly jazzed up version of "Just As I Am" as the ushers passed the bread and grape juice around. I would have preferred a heavily jazzed up version, but we have a number of elderly congregants. I'm pretty sure giving them a heart attack during communion would not endear me to… well, anyone.

We finished, finally, and made our way off-stage as Pastor B took the podium. I settled into the pew next to Zach as Pastor B opened his message in prayer.

"Almighty Father, we are in awe of your greatness. We praise you for your goodness to us, and we ask now that you would cause your Word to work within us and to accomplish that end for which you sent it into the world. In the precious name of your son, Jesus, Amen."

Pastor B has used the same opening prayer for as long as I can remember. To the word.

"I'd like to speak to you this morning on the subject of infinity," he started. "I think all too often, we approach faith, or the Bible, or even God himself assuming that we've seen all there is. That all excitement and surprise and, well, mystery is in the past. And the future is simply a rehashing of old ideas and rewalking of paths we've already tread."

Yup. Been there, done that. After seventeen-plus years in the pew, it didn't seem like there was a lot of new stuff Pastor B could dish out.

"But I'd like us to consider today that perhaps our image of God is simply smaller than it should be. Perhaps we've made him smaller than he is. Perhaps the God of the Bible is indeed far bigger and more mysterious than we've given him credit for. In my preparation for this week's message, I spent a lot of time in Romans 9. In this chapter, Paul writes to the church in Rome of the mystery of God's election. That from before the foundation of the world, God chose his elect from among the nations."

Admittedly, I was becoming interested in the message. On most Sundays, I tolerate the forty minute messages, counting down the seconds to the end of the sermon and my being freed to enjoy the rest of my weekend.

But this had me curious. Pastor B went on to talk about God's righteous election, how before the world itself was even created there were those selected for salvation, how the Potter had power over the clay to do what he wanted. It was confusing. I've heard people talk about "the elect" before, but I always thought it was just fancy language. A comparison, perhaps, to Israel being God's chosen people. But Pastor B was saying that God actually chose us from "before the foundation of the world."

That part sounded great, and it seemed to be the part

that Pastor B was intent on driving home. That God's irresistible grace meant that everyone he had chosen would be saved. But despite the overarching message of hope, I couldn't escape one horrifying conclusion.

If God could choose some to be saved, then why wouldn't he choose to save everyone? Was he actually choosing to set some people aside for eternal damnation?

And if everyone chosen would get saved, no matter what, did that mean that anyone not chosen would be damned, no matter what?

Pastor B didn't keep me in suspense for long.

"It's hard for us to comprehend," he admitted. "Our frail human minds rebel against the notion that a person can be destined from birth for an eternal judgment. We want to insist that such a thing would be the act of a cruel and heartless despot."

Um, yeah…

"But this only reveals the depth of our own depravity and the arrogance of man to suggest that our understandin' of what is right or good or just can override what God himself has determined. If God is good, and God is love, as Scripture clearly tells us, then when we read in Romans 9 that there are vessels of wrath fitted to destruction and that the Potter has power over the clay to make vessels unto honor and dishonor, we must conclude that these things are not incompatible with God's love and goodness. We are forced to confront the fact that our limited, flawed intellect cannot be trusted to make such determinations. We must humbly, gratefully come to the Word of God and submit ourselves to God as we find him there. And he is a great

God, an immense God far beyond our understandin'. We must never, ever try to force him to fit the requirements we may wish to set for him, but rather we ourselves must change to fit the requirements he has set for us."

He continued like that for another twenty-five minutes, building on the theme of God's mystery and the critical importance of approaching God in humility in light of how impossible it could be for us to understand him and his nature. "For my thoughts are not your thoughts," he quoted from Isaiah 55, "neither are your ways my ways, declares the LORD. As the heavens are higher than the earth, so are my ways higher than your ways, and my thoughts than your thoughts."

My mind reeled as I rose during his closing prayer and moved back to the piano. I played through "How Great Is Our God," my fingers set on autopilot. I'd heard these doctrines before, but I don't think they'd ever fully registered. It scared me because they made some degree of sense. If God created us, and if he is the final arbiter of what is right and good and whatever, then who am I to say otherwise?

But it just couldn't be true, could it? What could love mean if it included a God that would create a perfect, innocent little baby with the intent of burning that baby in hell forever? Especially if it meant that baby would never even have a real chance to choose God and be saved?

I tried to smile and say "Hi" to people after service had ended, but even with all my practice at forced emotion, I found it hard to act like nothing was wrong. I moved outside and slid around to the back of the building. There's an old metal ladder attached to the rear of the church that must have been intended as a fire escape. Years of renovations had rendered it almost useless, but it still provided quick access to the roof.

I scaled the wall and collapsed against a barrier toward the front of the building. I could hear people thirty feet below me milling around. Happy. Content. It seemed of the hundreds of people in attendance, I was the only one whose world had been shaken by what Pastor B had said. I could vaguely hear him greeting people and shaking their hands as they left. They in turn were thanking him for his message and saying how much it moved them and whatever. I had watched this scene play out countless times before, and it never varied in the slightest.

People find comfort in routine. I guess it helps them to make sense out of the world's inherent unpredictability.

I closed my eyes and tried to shut out the noise around me. I'd gone from wrestling with questions of sin and grace and repentance and pleasing God just two hours prior to asking some fundamental questions about God himself.

Chief among them was this: if God really was who Pastor B seemed to think, did I even want anything to do with him?

4

Confession: despite being seventeen years old, and decently good looking (I think), I'd spent most of my life up till senior year single.

And, yeah, by most, I mean all.

If teenage dating is an awkward concept under normal circumstances, then you can only imagine what it looks like in a Christian high school. Take a parental attitude of, "We'd prefer you didn't date, but won't actually tell you not to," combine it with a nebulous school policy that sort of did but sort of didn't frown on dating, and throw them both in a blender with every single Christian book on kissing dating goodbye or giving dating a chance or courting or arranging marriage or whatever… needless to say the whole concept of male-female relationships had become a hopeless quagmire, and it was way easier just to avoid the whole mess.

At least, that's what I told myself. Though it probably had as much to do with the fact that no sane girl had ever shown the slightest interest in me. I'd had my share of crushes, but nothing substantial enough to act on.

Cut to jazz band one Tuesday afternoon in late September. Mr. Ellis, our band instructor, subscribed to the least-common-denominator theory of band music. Essentially, take the least talented kid in class, pick a song he could handle and play decently well, and subject the entire band to it for however long it took. For that week, we were tortured with the saddest arrangement of "It Don't Mean a Thing (If It Ain't Got That Swing)" you've ever heard. I envied the marching band, which I'd heard was working on a medley of classic movie tunes. Hard to march with a piano, though.

Jazz band was fourth period, and given that it's a Tuesday-Thursday class, that made it the last hour and half of my day. As the brass warmed up, I was almost completely zoned out when the most beautiful creature Knight's Day had ever seen walked in. I'd never seen her before, and for a moment I felt convinced she'd entered the wrong room. Then I noticed she was carrying something that looked for all the world like a clarinet case. A few moments passed before I realized I was holding my breath. I forced myself to exhale slowly, hoping that I didn't look like a complete buffoon.

Mr. Ellis walked up to her and smiled before saying, "Class, I'd like to introduce Amelia Davidson. Her family has just moved here from…"

"Cleveland," she said.

I felt sorry for Cleveland. Their loss was undeniably our gain.

"Cleveland," Mr. Ellis echoed. "Anyhow, Amelia has been admitted to Knight's Day and will be joining our band as first clarinet."

Actually, she'd be joining our band as the only clarinet, but I wasn't going to quibble over details at a moment like this.

Mr. Ellis directed her toward an open seat and instructed the class to open our music books. I was already set and definitely not listening to Mr. Ellis. With as much nonchalance as I could I manage, I kept sneaking peaks in her direction. Her straight brown hair fell a few inches past her shoulders before curling out just a bit at the end. Her bangs were cut short, framing a face that could only be described as angelic. Up until that moment, I couldn't have imagined anything so stunning this side of heaven.

"Mr. Rudolph?"

Mr. Ellis had been trying to get my attention. "Perhaps we could trouble you to start us off?"

I breathed a silent prayer of thanks that Amelia had been busy with her clarinet and seemed unaware of my attention. I launched into the opening bars of the world's only arrangement of "It Don't Mean a Thing" that actually lacked swing. With the entire room now focused on the song, I was able to continue stealing glances in her direction. She knew her way around the clarinet.

Given my lack of experience in the girlfriend arena, I had no idea what to do. As we slogged through the swingless tune, I racked my brain trying to come up with a non-awkward way to meet her.

"Hi, I'm Rudy. I guess we'll be playing together."

Ouch. No.

"Hi, I'm Rudy. Welcome to Knight's Day."

Not bad, but really no where to go in the silence immediately following her, "Thanks," reply.

"Hi, I'm Rudy. I think you're gorgeous and would love to take you out for dinner."

Perhaps a little too on the nose.

It went back and forth like that for an hour and a half.

By the end of the period, the band had come close to achieving a mild swing, but it was still rather pathetic. Everyone filed out of the room, and I watched with no small degree of disappointment as Amelia collected her things and left. In the end, I hadn't come up with a single workable opening line, so I opted for the safe road.

Silence. Safe, unchallenging, unrewarding silence.

Sim had an after-school electronics club on Tuesdays and Thursdays, so I had an extra hour to kill before he'd be ready to leave. I looked at the music sitting in front of me and sighed. It just shouldn't be that hard to make this song *move*. That was, after all, the composer's original intent.

I thought about it for a minute and started playing again. At first, I stuck to the lines written in front of me. But heck, no one else was around, so I just let it go. Improvising, building, messing up here and there, but with no one around it hardly mattered.

I played that way for about ten minutes. And I have to say, it rocked more than a little. It Don't Mean a Thing had regained it's swing, and I decided I'd have to ask Mr. Ellis if we could switch things up a bit.

"Wow."

I turned to see who was eavesdropping on my private session, and my breath caught in my throat. Amelia Davidson was standing in the doorway.

"Did you come up with that on your own?" she asked.

Don't blow it, don't blow it, don't blow it...

"I guess, sort of. Felt like it was missing something so I started with what we had and tried to build on it a little. Figured it couldn't really get any worse."

A coherent sentence. Excellent!

She laughed. Nothing I produced on a keyboard had ever sounded as musical as her laugh. "I know, right? The admissions counselor warned me the jazz band wasn't anything amazing, but that was weaker than I expected. If everyone could play like you just did, though, we'd have some serious game."

I was dreaming. I must have fallen asleep waiting for Sim, and was dreaming. It was the only possible explanation for what was happening.

But I wasn't waking up.

"Thanks. It seemed like you had a better grasp of that than most of our bandmates," I said, gesturing at her clarinet case.

She blushed. "Oh, thanks. I guess as long as I've been playing I should have learned something by now."

"Been playing long?" I asked, begging God for this conversation to continue as long as possible.

She nodded. "Since I was six."

"How'd you settle on the clarinet?"

She blushed again. Amazing that a girl this gorgeous could seem as nervous as I felt.

"I liked the way the name sounded," she admitted.

I smiled. "Really?"

"Yeah. My mom gave me a list of instruments. Trumpet, trombone, saxophone…Eventually it came down to flute and clarinet. Clarinet sounded the prettiest, so that's what I picked."

"That's gotta be the greatest reason I've ever heard for why someone picked an instrument. My parents said I was going to learn the piano, period. I think they were thinking about a more classical direction. Jazz was my way of rebelling without rebelling."

She smiled, but said nothing. I feared the conversation was about to die and the glorious moment would end. "I'm Rudy, by the way."

She stepped forward and held out her hand. "Nice to meet you, Rudy. I guess you already know my name. But my friends call me Amy."

I shook her hand, trying to wrap my head around the fact that I was actually *touching* her. Did I dare take a chance?

What the heck? Caution is for sissies anyway.

"Can I count myself a part of that group?" I asked.

"Well, that depends," she said, a playful tone in her voice. "I have to drop off some papers at the main office to finalize my admission, and I have no idea where that is. A *real* friend would help me get there."

This. Can't. Be. Happening.

"Hm. I think I can manage that…Amy."

As we left the band room, I asked what brought her family from Cleveland. For a moment she fell quiet, and I feared I'd asked the wrong question.

"My dad died."

Doh.

"Oh, man. I'm sorry," I said, feeling like an idiot.

She smiled, though I suspected it was forced. "Don't worry about it. You couldn't have known. It happened about six months ago, so I'm past the initial wave. It took longer than we wanted to get everything in order and sell the house there. We moved here over the weekend to be closer to my mom's sister."

"Wow." I had a thousand other questions, but I wasn't sure which, if any, were okay to ask.

"Yeah, it sucks. But life goes on, you know? I did the whole grief-stricken-mess thing for a couple weeks, but eventually the sun rises again."

I nodded, imagining rather than understanding what she meant.

"What about you?" she asked. "How long have you lived in the Denver area?"

"Pretty much always. My folks lived in Texas until I was three, but I don't really remember it."

"You like it here?"

I shrugged. "Yeah, I guess. Haven't really known much else. But warm summers, snowy winters, any kind of outdoor or indoor activity you could want within a couple-hour drive…hard to complain."

"Yeah. I love the mountains. I can't wait to get out and do some hiking. More water sports than hiking or camping in Cleveland."

"Oh yeah? Where's the water in Ohio?"

"The Great Lakes. Cleveland sits right on the edge of Lake Erie. Gets pretty cold in the winters, but it can be fun in the summer."

If you'd told me twenty-four hours prior that the most exciting conversation of my day would revolve around Cleveland, I would have laughed. Hard. But here I was. Suddenly Cleveland sounded like the most interesting city in America.

We arrived at the office, and Amy dropped off her papers.

"My mom's waiting in the lot," she said. "I probably shouldn't keep her."

"Yeah. Guess I'll see you tomorrow?"

"You bet. See ya!"

And she was gone.

Three hours prior, Knight's Day Academy had seemed a dreary place to spend my senior year. Now I couldn't imagine any place I'd rather be.

5

My luck only got better on Wednesday. Of my five classes, Amy was in four. Of those four, she found an open desk next to mine in three.

And we had free period at the same time.

Given that she hadn't had time to make friends before our conversation on Tuesday, I was the only person in school she knew. I'd won the lottery.

"Well, that class should be easy for the next couple weeks," Amy said as we filed out of AmLit.

"Easy?" I asked. "And what, pray tell, do you find easy about *The Great Gatsby?*"

"It's my favorite book! I must have read it at least five times."

"Really? I haven't gotten past the first ten pages. What's so great about it?"

By now we'd made our way into the library, so she dropped her voice to just above a whisper.

"Well, I don't want to spoil it for you. It's…I don't know.

It's just so *full.* It's sad and dark in places, sure. But it's also beautifully true. It's like all of life wrapped into one small book."

I looked at her, an eyebrow raised.

"Fine, be a skeptic. You'll see."

Eyebrow still raised, I said, "I'll try to keep an open mind."

She smiled. Good grief, it's like the whole world stopped moving every time she did.

"Good. So, if not early-20th century American Literature, what kind of books do you read?" she asked.

"I like Grisham, some of Clancy's stuff." I wondered how much to admit to. "And I like some fantasy."

"*Some?*" she asked.

"Okay, fine. I love fantasy. Preferably futuristic, but medieval can work, too."

"So, what? Like *Lord of the Rings?*"

I shrugged. "*Lord of the Rings* is okay. I like the basic story of it, but Tolkien got bogged down in his own world-building. He was obsessed with languages and songs and poetry and a bunch of stuff that I think most people just skip right over. There's better stuff out there."

"Better than Tolkien?" she asked, incredulous.

"All right, *Gatsby* girl. I'll take it based on that little outburst that you've read the revered trilogy. Wait here a minute."

I got up and wandered through the shelves for a few minutes looking for the right book. I'd had to make a heck of a case to the librarian for why we should order it. In the end, I had to appeal on the basis of how difficult it is to get teenage boys to read. It took a couple months, but she relented.

I returned to our table, dropping it in front of her.

"*Mistborn?*" she asked. "Really?"

I nodded. "Really. All of the epic scale of Tolkien, better twists, a more compelling magic system, and none of the arduous songs or made up languages. I'm telling you, in fifty years people are going to be discussing Tolkien and Sanderson in the same breath."

"I think you're nuts."

"Probably," I said with a grin. "But nuts or not, it doesn't change the fact that this book is one of the best pieces of fantasy ever written. If you're going to insist that I keep an open mind about *Gatsby*, then you have to keep an open mind about this. Trust me.

"Okay," she relented, setting the book off to the side of the table.

We passed the whole hour like that, talking about our favorite books, movies, music, even video games.

"You're kidding," I said. "Call of Duty?"

"Oh my gosh, yes. Zombies more than anything. But Team Deathmatch is fun, too."

It was official. This girl was now without a doubt the most fantastic thing walking around Denver. Probably all of Colorado.

"My brother just got their new release," I said, more grateful than ever Zach had bought that Xbox. "You wanna come over after school and check it out?"

"Sounds great! I'll have to check with my mom first. You know how it is. New city, new school. After Dad, she's a little overprotective."

The bell rang, and we collected our things. Amy checked out *Mistborn*, and we headed for the cafeteria.

I was on cloud nine. Amy Davidson was going to spend the afternoon slaying zombies in my living room.

Life would be all downhill after that.

I'd filled Sim in on the previous day's happenings when he'd driven me home. He thought I was exaggerating when I told him how incredible Amy was. It was worth enduring his mocking disbelief to see his face now as he walked up to our lunch table. Amy was sitting across from me at an angle that prevented her from seeing him gape. He managed to regain control just before setting down his tray.

"Amy, this is Simon. Sim, Amy."

"Nice to meet you," Amy said, offering her hand.

Sim shook it. "You, too. Welcome to the purgatory that is Knight's Day Academy."

Amy laughed. "Oh, come on. It can't be that bad."

I grimaced. "He's not wrong. The opinion is pretty universal among the inmates. You'll feel the same way in another week or two."

"I don't know. The people at least seem more interesting than at my last school."

As far as I knew, she didn't really know anyone else but me yet. Point for Rudy.

"People, yes. Food, not so much," Sim complained as he sat on the bench next to me and began pushing some kind of green mush around his tray.

"That does look pretty grim," I admitted. "Forget your lunch?"

Sim shrugged. "Took a chance. Mom made pea salad last night, and she made sure to make plenty for leftovers. I gambled that whatever they were serving here today couldn't be that bad."

"Looks like you lost," Amy said.

I laughed. "No kidding. What is that?"

"Pureed green beans, I think. Who do you suppose decided it was appropriate to puree a vegetable for people older than nine months?"

"You got me, man. Your best option now? Eat the tots. Leave the puree. And pray your mom doesn't serve leftover pea salad for dinner."

Sim groaned. "It's sad how true that is. I may not survive. Surely circus people eat better than this. A diet of nothing but peanuts would be preferable."

Amy looked confused. "Say what?"

I rolled my eyes. "Sim's been planning his escape to the circus for the better part of four years now. You'll get used to it."

"I'm telling you, buddy, things keep going like they have the past week, and this is gonna be the year."

"Come on, Sim. As bad as Spanish II may be, you can't tell me you'd rather be shoveling elephant crap."

Sim made like he was thinking long and hard about it. "Maybe not," he finally admitted. "But they may wind up in a dead heat."

Amy laughed, then excused herself.

Sim lost no time. "Dude, you weren't lying."

I smiled, triumphant. "Told ya."

"And she's eating lunch with you?"

"Maybe more than that. I think she's coming over after school."

Sim about lost it. "Are you kidding!? How in the world did you swing that?"

"Apparently, she's into Call of Duty."

"Uh-uh. You're lying," he said, shaking his head.

I shook mine back at him. "She's particularly into Zombies."

His mouth fell open again. "Dude…"

"I know, man. I'm gonna wake up soon, I just know it."

"So, you gonna ask her out, or what?"

I shrugged. "Maybe. We'll see how things go this afternoon."

Sim took a breath and blew it out. "Well, good luck, man. You'd better move quickly, though. There's no way a girl like that's going to remain available for long."

Amy did succeed in getting her mom to let her come over for Zombies, but not by much. In the end, she only relented on condition that she would come and drive us to my house so she could meet me and Mom.

I'd stopped Zach in the hall outside of ninth-grade English and told him I needed to borrow his Xbox One after school. He was initially reluctant, and it ended up costing me a month of making his bed along with a solemn vow to leave his custom settings alone.

Totally worth it.

After school, we headed for the parking lot where Amy's mom was waiting beside a red minivan.

"Hi, Mom," Amy said, hugging her. "This is Rudy. Rudy, this is my mom, Claire."

I offered a hand. "Hi, Mrs. Davidson." Adults love it when you last-name them. "Nice to meet you."

"Nice to meet you, too, Rudy. I understand you're planning an afternoon of violence and gore?"

I froze. What the heck was I supposed to say to that?

"Um, well, we were planning on getting some homework done first, then we thought, maybe, when we were done we might, if it's okay with you that is…"

Claire started laughing. "They fall for it every time, don't they?"

Amy was laughing, too. "Yup. Almost too easy."

I chuckled nervously. "So, it's okay then?"

"Oh yes, Trevor loved that game. Spent hours playing. You don't think Amy just happened on to Call of Duty by accident, do you? She gets her love of undead combat straight from her father."

So, the world's most incredible girl apparently had one of the world's coolest moms.

"All right then," I said, unable to come up with anything else after getting so blindsided.

"Well, let's get going," Mrs. Davidson said, moving around to the driver's side. "Those zombies aren't going to dispatch themselves."

❖ ❖ ❖

That afternoon was incredible. For three glorious hours, we slew horde after horde of rampaging undead. And though I brought my A-game, those hours revealed an undeniable truth.

This girl was way better than me.

I got close in a couple rounds, but she had higher scores at the end of every single one. Headshots, total kills, combos…I couldn't touch her.

And she reveled in it.

After round one: "Boy, you just got walked all over by a girl."

And round five: "You're going to need some serious chiropractic work after that butt-kicking."

And round…twelve: "That's Amy: 12, Rudy: way less than 12."

Had it been Sim, I'd have gotten angry after three rounds. But each successive shellacking only increased the awe I held for Amelia Davidson. I thought about what Sim had said at lunch, that I'd better move quickly before she was off the market. But as we sat there, the game paused in the loading room, I couldn't bring myself to ask her. It just seemed too soon.

"Okay, so you have some natural aptitude for slaying the undead," I admitted. "Any other games at which you decimate unsuspecting victims?"

She shook her head. "I'm a one-genre girl. Give me guns and grenades and get outta my way."

I laughed.

I could hear voices coming from the other room. In the hours since we started playing, our moms hadn't stopped talking. Almost as soon as we arrived, Mom asked Claire if she and Amy wanted to stay for dinner. They'd been talking about who knows what ever since.

"Thirsty?" I asked.

"Parched."

We headed for the kitchen and the cans of soda stashed in the fridge. The moms were sitting in the dining room, the smell of an almost-finished pot roast starting to fill the house.

"You guys finished?" Mom asked.

I nodded. "My ego needed a break. Any more shots to the head and it wasn't ever gonna get up off the mat."

Claire laughed. "I thought about warning you, but it's so much funnier to let the guys get taken by surprise."

"Oh, I was surprised. By the way, you're on my team if we ever play 2v2 with Sim and Zach."

"That'd be fun," Amy said. "More victims for my assault rifle."

"What have you two been talking about?" I asked the moms.

"Oh, just about everything, really," Mom said. "We started with what brought them to Denver. Talked a bit about your dad, Amy. I'm so sorry. Then it was the school, and just now we were talking about church."

Claire nodded. "I thought we might go visit their church this Sunday, Amy. What do you think?"

Amy shrugged. "Sure. Might as well start where we know some people."

And now she was going to my church. If this got any more awesome my head was going to freaking explode.

"How long till dinner?" I asked.

Mom looked at the clock. "Should be ready to eat in about ten minutes. Your dad has a night class and your brother is eating at Steve's house, so it'll just be the four of us."

Aw, bummer.

We retreated back to the living room with our sodas. I collapsed on the couch and picked up a controller to shut off the Xbox. Amy fell into a recliner and set her soda on an end table. "So what kind of church do you go to?" she asked.

"It's called Riverside Christian. Pretty average, I guess. Non-denominational, pretty modern worship service, a few hundred people each week. Nothing revolutionary."

"Guess that goes for most churches," she said.

"Yeah?"

She raised her eyebrows. "You ever been to a church that you would describe as revolutionary?"

I shrugged. "Guess not. Haven't really been to that many churches. We've been going to RCC for as long as I can remember."

"Sounds nice. I've been in more churches than I can count."

"Why?"

She sighed, a long, tired sigh. "Dad was in the Coast Guard, so we moved every two or three years. Every new station meant a new church hunt, which meant Sunday after Sunday visiting churches where we didn't know anyone looking for one with the right mix of kids and adults and right doctrine and good worship…be glad you've never had to do that."

"Doesn't sound fun."

"You'd have a hard time making a bigger understatement. However unrevolutionary your church may be, I'm just glad I'll at least know someone there."

I smiled. "It'll be fun having you."

She seemed to soften at that. Her tone had taken on an edge ever since the topic of church came up.

She took another swig from her can.

"Do you not…*like* church?" I asked, somewhat surprised by my own audacity.

She looked at the TV, watching the No Signal sign bounce periodically around the screen. A few seconds passed before she said, "It's not that I *don't* like it. It's just that most of the time I don't really get it. I know the Bible says we should go to church, but so much of the time I'm not sure why. People there don't really seem much different from people anywhere else. Same dramas, same backbiting, same everything. And from one church to the next, no one can seem to agree on what to believe. Even within most churches you'll find different opinions on virtually everything. Post-trib rapture or pre-trib rapture? Sovereignty or free-will? To drink or not to drink? And it seems like no one can ever provide a better answer for why they believe what they believe than the next person. It just gets so confusing."

She paused. "Sorry. Guess I started ranting a bit, huh?"

I shrugged. "No big deal. I understand what you mean. I've wondered about some of that stuff lately, too."

"Yeah?"

"Sure. You just kinda wonder what to believe after a while."

She nodded. "That's it, exactly. I mean, I don't really buy evolution. That just seems like too much of a stretch. And it *feels* like Christianity is probably true. It just seems so hard to figure out what really *is* Christianity and what's stuff we've just made up."

I nodded, but didn't say anything further. I knew exactly what she meant and how it must make her feel. I thought about Pastor B's sermon on election for the thousandth time in three days. And I wondered how her dad dying factored into the whole thing. I had to imagine that would be one of her biggest questions. How could God let her dad die? I still didn't know how he died, but the how hardly seemed to matter. He was gone, and God could have stopped it. If Pastor B was right, God might have even caused it. How could she square with something like that?

I didn't feel comfortable enough yet to dig into such personal questions, but I made a mental note to ask her some other time.

Mom's head rounded the corner into the living room. "Soup's on!"

6

Sim wasted no time. First thing out of his mouth Thursday morning? "So, dude. You ask her out yet?"

When I said I hadn't, he spent the rest of the drive berating me for chickening out. I tried explaining that I just felt like it was too soon. We hadn't known each other long enough.

"Whatever, man. You got scared and bailed. Simple as that."

He wasn't wrong. I didn't want to risk whatever was happening. I'd known her for all of forty-eight hours, but I was falling hard. If I asked, and she said 'no,' things would get awkward. I couldn't risk that. I needed more time, and hopefully some kind of sign whether she had any feelings for me at all.

First class on the Tuesday-Thursday schedule is our mandatory Bible class. This semester's focus was church history, and as I dropped into my desk I thought about what Amy had said the day before. Church history was a garbage-pile mashup of people going to war over one belief or another. Inquisitions, crusades, dark ages, corrupt popes…and all of that piled on top of the pervasive doctrinal differences. How did anyone ever settle on what to believe?

Amy walked in two minutes before the bell and settled into the desk on my right. I told myself I would never again complain about our school's small size. Any bigger, and there's no way she and I would have had as many classes together as we did.

Bethany Waller, our Bible teacher, walked in thirty seconds before the bell and brought the class to attention. The school's disciplinary code helped ensure that once a teacher started talking, everyone else shut up.

"Good morning, class," she began. We echoed, though I doubted most of us felt it. "Today we'll begin talking a bit about your end-of-term assignments. I know it may seem like we're a long way off from December, but this particular project will likely require more time and research than what you may be used to."

A collective groan rose from the room, and Ms. Waller smiled.

"Yeah, I expected that. But don't worry. I'm a benevolent tyrant, and I want this exercise to be fun as well as challenging."

Right…

"Mr. Langford, could you come up here please?"

Sim looked stricken, like he was in trouble for something. He relaxed when Ms. Waller handed him a stack of papers to pass out to the class.

"The sheet you receive from Mr. Langford will contain

three or four lines about a mystery person that made a lasting contribution to the history of our faith. Part one of your job is to identify the person described by the facts on your sheet. Yes, Mr. Young."

Someone had raised a hand. No one spoke in Ms. Waller's class without raising a hand first.

"So, it's like Jeopardy: Church History Edition?"

Ms. Waller smiled. "Exactly. Now, I think we have far more to learn from these people than the biographical headlines that tend to monopolize this sort of assignment, so we're going to do things a little differently. While you can certainly make reference to the facts on your sheet in the final paper, you are forbidden from focusing on them. For instance, if your sheet says, 'Helped orphans in China," you must *focus* on some other aspect of the subject's life. I want you to really learn about your person beyond what history has focused on. And then I want you to write three thousand words about how that person's life affects you on a personal level. I want you to be honest and open with this assignment. I want to know how what you learn about these people's lives *moves* you. Your papers will be due on my desk by the end of the second Thursday in December."

I was surprised. She'd managed to make it sound *not* totally boring. I flipped over the sheet Sim had handed me and read through the facts:

- Father of the Methodist Church
- Preached in America from 1736-1737
- Persecuted by the Church of England

It wasn't a lot to go on, but I suspected a quick Google search for "Father of the Methodist Church" would tell me what I needed to know.

The rest of the class was a rather forgettable discussion of Martin Luther's early life. Medieval fantasy could be interesting. Medieval history? Not so much.

As we rushed out after the bell, Sim, Amy, and I huddled around our sheets. Sim had already whipped out his smartphone and was busy looking up who he had. His facts were:

- Played professional baseball
- Left baseball career to work for the YMCA
- Preached to over 100,000,000 people during his life

It didn't take more than a few minutes for him to say, "Aha! Got it! Billy Sunday. Played for the Chicago White Stockings before getting saved and quitting the team to work for the YMCA in Chicago."

"Figures you'd get the athlete," I said, not bothering to hide my jealousy.

"What's yours say, Amy?" Sim asked.

She looked at her sheet. "Wrote one of the most famous devotional books in history, worked as a chaplain in Egypt during World War I, died of appendicitis because he didn't want to take a hospital bed from a wounded soldier."

"Hmm," Sim said, turning back to his phone. "Here you go," he said a few minutes later. "A little harder to find than the baseball player. You've got Oswald Chambers. The devotional mentioned is "My Utmost for His Highest.""

"My parents have that book," I said. "I've seen it on my

dad's nightstand a few times."

"I've heard of it," Amy said, "but I haven't ever read it. Guess that'll change this year. What about you, Rudy? Who'd you get?"

I read off my facts, and Sim went to work. Mine took less time than either of theirs.

"John Wesley," he announced. "An Anglican preacher born in 1703. Started the Methodist church and it looks like the powers that be weren't too happy about it."

"Thrilling. You get the baseball player, Amy gets the guy who died of appendicitis, and I get some guy who apparently lived in England three hundred years ago and started a denomination. I don't suppose either of you wanna trade?"

Sim shook his head. "Sorry, dude. Not a chance."

"Nah," Amy said. "Sorry, but I'm actually kind of interested in what else this Chambers guy did besides write the book."

"Yeah," I said. "I didn't think so."

Saturday morning, I paid a little more attention than usual to worship practice. When a girl you're trying to impress is going to be in the congregation, it's only natural that you take extra precautions to not look like a complete fool.

It seemed like eons had passed since I'd met Amy, and I was surprised to realize we'd only known each other for four days. We'd hung out almost all day, every day at school, and she had come over for Zombies again after school on Friday. Now that her mom had been assured we weren't psychopaths, Amy had been allowed to come over unattended. After that, I owed Zach two months of bed making and a week of laundry. I was going to have to come up with another arrangement, or the rest of my life would be spent in service to my kid brother.

Saturday was the first day since we'd met that I wasn't going to see her. As soon as worship practice was over, I found I had no idea what to do with my time. All I wanted was to be with her, but try as I might I couldn't come up with a single reason to call her that wouldn't come off as desperate.

So, I went home and paid half-hearted attention to my homework. History was boring, Amy was captivating. Math was drudgery, Amy was exhilarating. Biology was bland, Amy was beautiful.

The work slowly got done, but I could never really get focused on it. Amy had invaded my mind and taken up what might be permanent residence there. Everything else was getting crowded to the edges.

I was halfway through my required reading on Luther's nailing of the Ninety-Five Theses to the church door when Dad called from the other room, "Rudy! Telephone!"

I figured it must be Sim, probably as bored as I was. I found Dad in the kitchen, and he handed me the phone.

"Hi, this is Rudy."

"Rudy! I hoped this was your number."

Amy...

"Hi, Amy. How'd you find it?"

"Phone book. There's a bunch of Rudolphs, but the addresses are listed, too. I hope this isn't, like, creepy-stalkerish. But I'm really bored. You wanna do something?"

Hmm. Learn about the start of the Protestant Reformation, or spend a sunny Saturday afternoon with Amy Davidson?

"Sure!" I said, trying not to sound as excited as I felt. It wasn't easy. "You have something in mind?"

"I don't know. It's a nice day outside. You have a car, right?"

"Sorta, yeah."

"I've heard a lot about the 16th Street Mall. We could go there and walk around. Or whatever. I'm not really picky. The walls are just starting to close in, and I still don't really know anyone other than you and Sim."

I would have preferred the reason be that she couldn't bear to be apart from me for a whole day, but what the heck? I'd take whatever the universe offered.

"Sure, that works. I can leave here in a few minutes. You want me to pick you up at home?"

She gave me her address, which turned out to be just a five or six minute drive from mine. We hung up, and I bolted for my keys.

Denver's 16th Street Mall has never had much appeal for me. I'm a guy, and no one's ever going to accuse me of having a sharp sense of style. So most of the apparel-type shops that comprise the Mall don't really appeal to me.

On the other hand, Amy was nothing if not appealing. And if she wanted to go to the 16th Street Mall, then I wanted to go, too.

I pulled into her driveway nine minutes and twenty-eight seconds after we'd hung up the phone. She was wearing jeans and a T-shirt featuring some band I'd never heard of.

I'd opted for blue jeans and a graphic tee under an open button-up. I really had no idea what to wear, but I'd seen pictures of guys dressed like this, and they always seemed to look cool. As Amy slid into the passenger seat, I envied her a bit. What must it be like to look amazing no matter what you wore?

"Nice car," she said with a hint of sarcasm.

"Hey now," I said, feigning offense. "Watch it. Otis may be an old soul, but he gets the job done."

She laughed. "You named your car Otis?"

I shrugged. "Seemed appropriate."

"All right then, Otis." She patted the dashboard. "Take us away."

We eased out of the driveway and headed downtown. The Mall was about twenty-five minutes away from where we lived.

"So, boring Saturday, huh?"

"Yeah," she said. "Since it's just me and Mom, weekends are a lot quieter than they used to be. I tried doing some homework, but I got stir crazy pretty quick."

I nodded. "I know the feeling. And it's way too nice a day to waste on homework."

"Oh, I know," she said rolling down her window. She stretched as the wind tousled her hair. "Cleveland could get so humid in the late summer. The first few weeks of school were always pretty miserable. But the air here is so fresh."

"I guess," I said. "I've never really noticed."

"People take for granted what they have. You should travel sometime. Getting around to other places would give you a new appreciation for what you have here."

"I'd like to. I've always thought about traveling, but my parents are homebodies. We've never gone much of anywhere."

Amy looked aghast. "Yeah? Where do you guys vacation?"

"Mostly just here," I admitted. "We've gone down to Colorado Springs and the Garden of the Gods, or up to Estes Park. We'll visit the mountains for camping in the summer or skiing and snowboarding in the winter. But Mom and Dad's parents both lived here, so our family is all nearby. Just wasn't ever much reason to go anywhere else I guess."

"You've never even been out of state?" she asked, her unbelief growing.

"Oh, I have. A couple times. We visited the Grand Canyon one summer, and another year we made it up to Mount Rushmore. But that's about it."

"Wow. I don't even know what to say to that." Then, in direct contradiction to her previous statement, she declared, "You've been sheltered."

I shrugged. "I try to compensate where I can. In fact, my imagination just spent several nights on Long Island in the 1920s."

"You read *Gatsby*? All of it?"

I nodded. "It was a grind to get through the first twenty pages or so, but it picked up a bit after that."

"So, what'd you think?" she asked, her excitement evident.

"To be honest it was kind of depressing. I can't say I see what you found so engrossing about it."

She sighed. "Well, I admit my reasons for liking it are probably not the same reasons other people have. I like it because it's the only book I've ever found that seems to understand life and the way people really are. You remember the first scene where Nick goes over to Daisy's house for tea?"

"Sure."

"You remember what Daisy said she wished for her daughter?"

"Not really," I admitted with a grimace. "Sorry."

She closed her eyes and thought for a moment. "'I'm glad it's a girl. And I hope she'll be a fool - that's the best thing a girl can be in this world, a beautiful little fool.'" She finished the quote and opened her eyes.

"So, she wanted her daughter to be as vapid and airheaded as she was. And...you like that *why*?" I asked.

"Ugh, men!" she said. "Do you really not see it?"

It took me a second to get past the fact that she considered me a man rather than a boy, but I recovered and said, "Sorry. It just seems pointless. What's the sense in going through life a fool? And wanting that for your children? I think I'd want my kids to see the world for what it is and act...I don't know. Wisely, I guess."

"But that's just the thing," Amy insisted. "Her wish of foolishness for her daughter is actually one of the most profound moments in the book. Think about the characters.

With the exception of Nick, who I think is probably the only really honest character in the book, everyone, including Gatsby, is really a terrible person. Tom is cheating on his wife. Mrs. Wilson is cheating on her husband. Mr. Wilson is a crazed murderer. Jordan is a cynical cheat and a liar. Gatsby is trying to steal another man's wife. And Daisy cheats on her husband. The world of *Gatsby* is chock full of people who act only in their own self-interest. Which I guess is to say, it's full of people that are just like real people."

"Okay," I said. "I'm with you so far."

"Take Tom for instance. He seems to have no problem with his own infidelity, but he freaks out when Daisy has the audacity to cheat on him. It's inconsistent and unfair. And Daisy, she can't decide if it's better to go with a new love or a lifetime commitment she's already made. People constantly act in contradiction to what they say they believe. Sound familiar?"

I nodded. "You're referring to our conversation the other day? About the church?"

"Exactly!" she said, excited that I might finally be getting it. "In a world where people can't even act true to their own belief systems, the only way to make sense out of life is to not try. To be foolish and ignorant that anything of significance is happening beyond the next outlandish party. That's what Daisy wished for her daughter: the bliss of ignorance. In a way, that wish made her the most insightful person in the entire story."

And with that, Amy Davidson became the most insightful person in mine.

❖ ❖ ❖

I had to admit, with Amy's exposition of its virtues, *Gatsby* had suddenly become a far more interesting book than I'd realized. It was going to make my reflection paper a *lot* easier to write.

And once again, I was in awe of this girl that was well on her way to becoming one of my closest friends. We talked about *Gatsby* the rest of the way to the Mall. She loved the language of the era. I liked the idea of frequent late night parties. To hear my parents tell it, all civilized people always went to bed at a reasonable hour. F. Scott Fitzgerald, on the other hand, seemed of the opinion that normal folks partied until dawn on the weekends. I tucked that tidbit away for the next time I needed an excuse to stay out late.

We got to the mall, spent just shy of an eternity finding a parking spot, and walked around for over an hour. Amy went in almost every clothing store we came to. In every shop, she'd find something out of the ordinary, model it for me, and ask, "You think this is something Daisy would wear?" Half the time the answer was yes. Half no. But Amy looked amazing in all of it.

By mid-afternoon, we were both a bit tired, hot, and ready for a break. We headed into a pizza place and split a medium. Half Canadian bacon and pineapple (for me) and half pepperoni and black olives (for her).

Midway through my second slice, I said, "I'm curious. The people in *Gatsby* are almost universally screwed up. Even Nick, who's pretty solid, ends up a cynic at the end of it because of how screwed up everyone else is. Do you think things are anywhere near that bad among Christians?"

Amy chewed, thoughtfully, polishing off the last bit of her first slice. She leaned back, as though the subject itself was exhausting. "I don't know. Maybe, I guess. I haven't really seen much to convince me otherwise."

"What *have* you seen?"

"A lot of the same stuff as you, I would guess. Remember that pastor, from here in Colorado I think? It was a few years back now. He was president of some big conservative organization and it was reported that he was doing drugs and having sex with a male prostitute."

I nodded. It had been a big deal at our church when it happened, especially given that the church the man pastored was only about an hour away from us.

"I mean, here was a man that preached against homosexuality, yet engaged in it himself. Seems a lot like Tom, having his own affair while preaching about the values of Daisy staying at home and not fooling around on him." She paused. She picked an olive off the pizza tray and stared at it as though it alone held the key to understanding such things. Popping it in her mouth, she resumed. "I mean, that's a huge, public example of what I mean. But think about it. Have you ever known anyone in any church anywhere that seemed at all different from anyone in the world?"

I thought about it. Our church was small and relatively calm, but just a year ago there had nearly been a split in the church over a proposed remodel. About half the folks involved thought we should get new, more modern style chairs. The other half thought the pews were just fine and said the money should be spent on new carpeting. My parents felt it was our responsibility to be at all such business meetings, and I remember the raised voices and anger in the faces of many of the people present. If I hadn't been sitting in church, I wouldn't have had any reason to think that those people were Christians. Even my parents, who were good people, didn't seem that far removed from people outside the church. They were nice enough, but I'd known non-Christians who were nice. What was the difference?

"I guess I haven't," I admitted.

Amy nodded, unsurprised. "The only exception to this I've ever come across is my mom. I mean, she's not perfect. But after my dad died, I expected her to rail against God. You know, to blame him for what happened. But she never did. She cried, sure. She grieved for weeks, months even. I remember overhearing conversations with her friends when she would ask things like, 'How do I make sense of this?' But never for a moment did she seem to waiver in her faith. It was inspiring, but in my experience that kinda thing is the exception rather than the rule."

I nodded. "More and more lately, I've been wondering about the whole thing. Last week, Pastor B was talking about election. He said before people are even born God has decided if they're going to heaven or hell. People don't even get a chance to choose. It's already determined for them before they commit a single sin. He's also told me that God doesn't expect us to be perfect. Just sorry or repentant after we sin. So, it doesn't seem like we're really expected to act any different as Christians. Just be sorry here and there. It all seems so arbitrary, doesn't it?"

Amy nodded. "The churches I've been in have taught the same thing. And it's not just whether we go to hell or not. It's everything. They teach that we're responsible for our choices, but ultimately it's God that decides everything that happens. It's one of those mysteries that we're supposed to take on faith is just how it is."

I couldn't make sense of it. "So, God decides things are going to be a certain way, we can't choose otherwise, but we're responsible for our choices and either punished or rewarded for them? How does this make sense?"

She shrugged. "I don't know. I've been wrestling with it ever since my dad died. My dad was part of a marine rescue unit. They were out trying to help a yacht stranded in a storm. People who should have known better were too stupid to check a weather report before heading out for a pleasure cruise. My dad went out to try to save them, and he did. The stupid people all lived. He didn't. And I'm supposed to believe that God decided it was supposed to happen that way. If that's true, I'm not sure I care for God at all."

She hesitated, and looked a bit scared. Like she was afraid she'd gone too far.

I nodded. "I know what you mean. I mean, not about your dad. I can't imagine what that must be like. But I know what you mean about God. How are we supposed to reconcile a loving God deciding to send people to hell when they haven't even done anything wrong yet?"

Amy smiled, but her eyes didn't. "I don't know. But I'm glad I finally have someone I can talk to about it. I tried talking to Mom after Dad died. She'd just say, 'God is bigger than we are, sweetheart. He's infinite. How could we hope to understand this? We just have to trust him, that when he says he loves us, he really does.' But the questions haven't gone away. And I don't know that I can just believe like she does."

"Me either. So, where does that leave us?"

She shook her head. "I don't know." She was silent for moment, then added, "At least we're not alone, I guess."

Her hands were on the table, barely six inches from mine. I decided to cross the Rubicon, and slowly reached out to take her hand.

She didn't draw back. She opened her hand and accepted mine.

And we just sat there, holding hands, for what seemed like forever.

7

As we walked back to the car hand in hand, I couldn't imagine a greater high. And granted, I had no frame of reference for this sort of thing, but I was pretty certain I was in love with her.

We drove home in relative silence. I had one hand on the wheel, but my other hand refused to let go of her. She didn't seem in any hurry to let go, either. We'd found something precious, someone who understood these critical parts of us. Our doubts, our fears. We kept silent, as if afraid that any sound might break the moment's spell.

We pulled into her drive just before six, and I put Otis in park. I looked at her, and she looked back at me. I don't know how long we sat that way before she said, "Thanks for taking me to the Mall. I…I had a great time."

"Me, too," I said, unable to think of anything else.

"See you tomorrow, then?" she said.

"Yeah, see you at church."

Neither of us moved, our hands still connected.

She smiled. "I really should go. Mom's expecting me in there for dinner."

"Right," I said, blushing a bit. I slowly let go of her hand, and she slid from the car.

Leaning back in, she said, "You're something, Mr. Rudolph. You know that?"

If my heart pounded any harder, it was going to explode out of my chest. "I don't know. But you're amazing, Miss Davidson."

She smiled. "Good night." She closed the door, and I watched as she walked away. She turned and waved at me from the door, biting her lower lip as she smiled.

Then she went inside, closed the door, and was gone.

I drove home in a daze, trying to process everything that had happened over the past week. I don't think I stopped smiling the whole way home.

As I walked in, Dad was setting the table while Mom pulled some kind of chicken out of the oven. I could hear Zach's Xbox. He'd apparently relocated it to his bedroom.

"Hey, just in time," Dad said. "How was your afternoon?"

I swallowed, trying to not look as giddy as I felt. "Good. You?"

"It was pretty quiet. Mowed the lawn. You go somewhere with Sim?"

I thought about lying. Dad had never expressly forbidden me to date, but he'd made it clear that he wasn't a fan of the idea. Lying might be easier, but when in doubt...

"Nah, I took Amy to the 16th Street Mall."

Dad paused, a plate hovering in his hand an inch or two

off the table, and raised an eyebrow. "Amy, huh? The young lady that was over yesterday?"

I nodded. "Yeah. She's new in town and doesn't know very many people yet."

"I see," Dad said. "It was just the two of you?"

I didn't like where this was going. "Yeah, we walked around for a bit and grabbed some pizza."

"Sounds like a date."

I shrugged, trying to downplay it as much as I could. "Maybe. I didn't really think of it like that. We were both a bit bored and decided to do something together. Is that a date?"

Dad resumed setting the table. "Single guy, single girl, hanging out and eating alone. Seems an awful lot like a date."

"Well, would that be a problem?" I asked. I could feel my frustration level rising, and it was getting hard to keep it out of my voice.

Dad shrugged. It was clear from the look on his face that regardless of what he said next, it was indeed a problem.

"She's an attractive young woman."

Yeah, noticed that.

"If you have feelings for this girl," he continued, "and you start getting close to her, you're going to want to act on those feelings. There's a physical component there that's strong, and it's hard to control. I'm not sure you're ready for that at 17."

What I wanted to say was, "Well, I am," but that wouldn't end well.

"Are you telling me to stop hanging out with her?" I

asked.

"Would you stop if I did?"

He caught me off guard with that. We didn't get that direct with each other. Ever since the night he hadn't come home, our relationship had been an elaborate dance around what we both really thought.

"I don't know," I said. "I wouldn't want to. I like her. We have a lot in common."

"Then I'll just say this. Be careful. You're in no position yet to make any kind of a commitment to this girl. Do you think you have any right to her heart until you are?"

Her heart? Good grief, Dad, it was one pizza.

"I'll be careful," I said, dodging his last question. The truth was she already had my heart, right or no right. And I wanted nothing more than to make her happy. How dangerous could that be?

"Dinner's ready," Mom announced.

"I'm not really hungry, and I've still got some homework stuff to get done. Can I be excused?"

Dad didn't look happy about it, but he gave a terse, "Sure."

I retreated to my room and started working through my Church History text, but I only made it a paragraph or two before my thoughts drifted back to Amy. It wasn't even worth trying to deny any more. I loved her, and I wanted nothing more than to spend every possible moment with her. We were both Christians. We both felt the same way about faith and apparently each other. And this was dangerous? Really?

But I didn't want the fight, so I decided to spend as

much time with her as possible while keeping it out of Dad's way. What he doesn't know, right?

Sunday morning was fantastic. I managed to not make an utter fool of myself in front of Amy, and she and her mom sat with us at church. We decided against holding hands in front of our parents, but she kept nudging mine when it seemed no one was looking. I nudged back, and we occupied ourselves with our little back and forth through an otherwise bland sermon about tithing. Pastor B gave one every six months or so, and it was always a major snooze.

Mrs. Davidson said the service was wonderful and the people were all nice, and she complimented my performance. I smiled and thanked her. Always nice to score points with your girl's mom.

It was amazing how fast it'd come to feel that way. That Amy Davidson was *my girlfriend*. We hadn't actually talked about it yet, and something told me that soon we were going to need to have an actual conversation about it. That wasn't going to be awkward at all.

Mom and Dad invited the Davidsons to join us for lunch. Once a month or so, we go to this little diner about a mile from the church for burgers after service. It's one of those greasy hole-in-the-wall joints that had somehow stumbled onto the magic recipe for the world's greatest bacon cheeseburgers. I must have had bacon cheeseburgers at just about every place in Denver that serves them, and at most places it wouldn't matter whether they put bacon on the burgers or not. You just can't taste it. I don't know why it's different at the Mile-Hi Diner. Maybe it has something to do with the kind of bacon they use, but the flavor just explodes from the burger. If I ever end up fat, I expect 60% of the blame to rest with every pizza joint in town, with the remaining 40% owing to the Mile-Hi's bacon cheeseburgers.

I may have been imagining it, but it seemed like Dad was maneuvering to position himself between Amy and me. As though he feared if I stood too close to her we might accidentally fall in love.

Too late, Dad.

We ate, and everyone raved about the food. I'd found it a universal reaction. If I ever meet a person who doesn't like these burgers, I'm gonna have to check him for a pulse.

Then came the worst part of the day. After lunch, the Davidsons went home, and I couldn't concoct a single excuse to stay with Amy.

It was probably just as well. In the previous evening's daze, I hadn't managed to make any headway with my remaining homework, and Church History was calling. As boring as the material was, it demanded my attention. I'd heard that most kids struggle in Ms. Waller's class, but I've long been convinced that's only because they don't bother with the homework. It's not like I'm obsessed with my grades or anything, but as long as I have to be in school, I might as well learn something while I'm at it.

The remainder of the afternoon was spent on homework and attempting to improve my zombie-slaying acumen. I'd reached an understanding with Zach. He would turn 16 in a month, and in exchange for my being allowed to use his

Xbox whenever he wasn't using it, he would be able to use Otis whenever I wasn't using it. As long as he chipped in for gas, that is. On the whole, he may have gotten the better end of the bargain. But I got access to the Xbox, a perpetual excuse to invite Amy over, and I no longer had to make his bed or do his laundry. All wins in my book.

Monday morning dawned, and for the first time in recent memory I couldn't wait to get to school. I was downstairs a solid fifteen minutes earlier than normal and drove myself to school. I'd called Sim to let him know.

"Need your own set of wheels today, eh?" Sim prodded.

"Never know," I said, refusing to commit. He'd know the truth soon enough, and again, I wanted to see the look on his face.

Of course, the problem with being really excited to get to school is that almost no one else feels the same way. So when you arrive to school a full thirty minutes before classes start, it's just you, the teachers, and the janitor wrapping up his buffing of the tile floors.

Part of me, a very large part, wanted to just sit and watch the parking lot for Mrs. Davidson's van. But the voice of my better angel shouted down that idea as more than a little desperate. I wandered instead to the jazz room and puttered around the piano.

"Hey, you," Amy said, arresting my attention from the keys. "Thought you might be in here."

I smiled and shook my head. "We've known each other a week, and I'm already predictable?"

"I'm a woman. We understand men," she said, half-kidding, as she rounded the piano and sat down on the bench next to me.

I started playing again, something easy that didn't require much of my attention. "Too bad that doesn't work both ways," I said, also half-kidding.

Amy raised an eyebrow at me. "Hey, now. As women, we're expected to shave our legs, we carry and give birth to children, and it takes us on average four or five times as long to get ready for our days as it does for men. You don't get to understand us. It's only fair."

It took everything in me to move past the mental image of Amy shaving her legs. I swallowed hard, nodded, and said, "I'll buy that."

"Class starts in five. You wanna walk me to Algebra?" she said, effecting a pleading expression that made her look adorable.

More than just about anything.

I took her hand as we headed out of the jazz room. Just because we didn't want to flaunt anything in front of our parents didn't mean I wasn't going to take every other opportunity to be as close to Amy as I could.

As we approached the classroom, I spotted Sim running in the school's main door. He was so focused on getting to class on time that he almost missed us walking toward him. He stood agape for just a moment, then pursed his lips in a semi-mocking half-grin, cocked his head, and gave a golf clap.

"Nice, dude," I said as we walked up to him. "Subtle *and* classy."

Fortunately, Amy seemed to take it in stride. "Come on, Rudy," she said. "Your friend can't congratulate you on holding hands with the pretty new girl?"

I shrugged and smiled. "I guess so."

As long as that's how she saw it, then by all means, Sim, clap away.

At lunch, Sim made himself scarce. I think he'd planned on sitting with us, but as he entered the lunch hall I shook my head. He gave a slight nod and a smile letting me know he understood.

I didn't like how nebulous my relationship was with Amy. We'd been holding hands like we were surgically attached all day, but we had yet to utter a single sentence about our actual status. Part of me was scared of wrecking whatever this was before it even started, but I figured there had to be at least part of her that was asking the exact same question…

What are we exactly?

"So," I said as we set our trays down.

"So," she said back.

"I'm sorry if this comes off as cheesy or dumb or whatever, but I honestly have no idea how these things are supposed to work. So, I'm just gonna ask. Do you want to be my girlfriend?"

She smiled. It seemed half in amusement at my awkwardness and half in real happiness that I'd asked.

"I kinda figured the hand-holding gave it away," she said.

A good answer, but still not clear.

"So, that's a yes?"

"Yeah, Rudy. That's a yes."

"Ok, then."

She laughed. "You're cute when you're uncomfortable."

I flashed a self-deprecating grin. "I must be really cute then."

"You have your moments."

I had a thousand questions I wanted to ask her now, but I figured Google might be a better choice for "How to be a good boyfriend?" and "How does a relationship work?" I breathed a silent prayer of thanks that I seemed to have a pretty understanding girlfriend. For the time being, I figured I'd just keep on keepin' on.

"Do you think there are answers to the questions?" Amy asked out of the blue.

"Which questions?"

"You know, the God questions. Do you think there are actually answers, or are we supposed to live in the grey?"

I thought for a minute, then shook my head. "I don't know. I guess people think the Bible says these things pretty clearly, but it's all just so hard to believe. So *wrong*. Maybe I'm 'putting myself above God' or something, I don't know. Until now, I never really had anyone I could talk to about it."

"You can't ask your Dad?"

I shook my head. "Dad doesn't really approve of doubt. Where do you think I first heard about 'putting myself above God?' Dad sees stuff like that as a lack of faith, or even arrogance to think I know better than the Almighty. And Mom goes along with Dad. She believes what he believes. Anytime I've ever asked her anything about God beyond something really basic, her response has been, 'Ask your father'."

"So, your Dad doesn't really allow doubt and our moms don't get it. Have you tried talking to your pastor?"

"Not really," I admitted. "It's only been here lately that these questions have really started bugging me. But I can't imagine him giving answers any different from what I've gotten from Dad. Especially after the sermon I told you about. He seems pretty set that we just have to believe this because it's what the Bible says."

Amy looked distant for a minute. "Hmm…"

"What?"

She didn't answer right away. "You said your pastor said we have to believe these things because it's what the Bible says." She said this in a measured tone, as if weighing each word carefully before letting it loose into the wild. "But, does it really?"

I shrugged. "I think so. I've read through a lot of the passages Pastor B referenced in that sermon. The Bible does talk a lot about predestination and God choosing us and stuff. What else could it mean?"

Amy shook her head, as if trying to dismiss a thought that refused to go away. "I don't know. But now that I think about it, I'm kinda wondering if the Bible really says what we've been told it says. I've had these questions even since before Dad died, and they've hounded me since then. But I've always just *assumed* that people were right when they said that this is what the Bible teaches. I don't think I've ever *really* looked into it before."

I raised an eyebrow. "You think all of these people in my family, your family, my church, and all of the churches you've been to...you think they've gotten it *wrong*?" The question came out a little more dismissively than I meant.

Amy looked a little deflated. "Like I said, I don't know. But is it really so outrageous to think that they might have gotten it wrong? It's not like it'd be the first time. We've been reading about Luther for Church History. The Catholic church was screwing things up for hundreds of years before he tacked his challenge to that door."

"So, what?" I asked. "This is all just a little bit of history repeating? You'd think if we could figure that out someone else would have by now."

"Why?"

I hesitated. "'Cause."

"'Cause why?"

"Because we can't be the first people to ask these questions!"

"Obviously," she allowed. "But who says the answers they came up with were the right ones? Don't you want to know for yourself?"

Now that the question had been raised, I knew it wouldn't go away. My need to know, like, *know* know had kicked in, and I knew I'd have to start digging.

"Yeah. I guess I kinda have to now."

"Do you mean that?" someone asked behind me.

The sudden introduction of another voice in the conversation startled me, and I jumped. I turned to see who had invaded our privacy and saw the gaunt form of Mark Behar sitting at the table behind us.

"Sorry, didn't mean to startle you. Or eavesdrop. But your conversation was intriguing."

"You think so, huh?" I said, my frustration at the violation seeping into my words. I didn't know Mark at all beyond a few classes we shared here and there. We'd never hung out.

"Yeah, I do. Do you both mean what you said? Do you really want to know for yourselves what the Bible says about those questions?"

I glanced at Amy, but she looked as confused as I felt. The conversation was getting weird.

"I guess so," I said. "What's it to you?"

"Well, I don't know exactly what questions you guys are asking, but I'm guessing they're not too different from the ones I've been wrestling with. If you're planning on really going after answers, I'd love to join you."

Amy and I looked at each other. She shrugged.

"I…guess so?" I said. I hadn't intended for it to come out sounding like a question, but I hadn't been prepared for an addition to this nascent endeavor, either.

"Great!" Mark said. "When do you plan to start?"

I almost shot back that he'd interrupted us before we had time to make any plans at all, but instead managed, "I don't know. We just now decided to do this. And it's not just the when, but the where that we need to figure out. Can't exactly hold a meeting like this at one of our houses."

"Agreed," Mark said. He pulled a notebook from his backpack and ripped out a piece of paper. As he scribbled on it, he said, "Here's my phone number. Give me a call when you decide what to do?"

"Sure." I was still uncertain about Mark, but he seemed sincere. And given the amount of study and research this project might require, it probably wouldn't hurt to have a third person on board.

Mark got up. "Well, I guess I'll be seeing you."

"Later."

He walked off, and Amy and I turned back to each other.

"That was…unexpected," she said.

"To say the least. I guess whatever we decide to do, we'll have company."

8

You'd think having an amazing girlfriend would provide a solid incentive to swear off the SD cards. And you'd be right. I wanted to be done with them. I'd taken a bunch out from where they were stashed in my dresser and pitched them. But one or two managed to survive. And wanting to stop doing something is not the same thing as actually stopping. I tried. I failed.

I watched.

Lying in bed that night, I wondered about what we would find when we started digging through the Bible. For years, I'd been sleepwalking through faith, just going with the theological flow created by people around me. Now that approach was generating more questions than answers. If we looked for ourselves, was the whole thing going to prove impossibly complicated, or was it possible that we might find more satisfying answers?

I wondered. And wrestled. Answers sounded good, but I wasn't sure I actually wanted them anymore. If it turned out that Christianity wasn't true, my life would get way easier. For starters, I'd get both my Saturday and Sunday mornings back. That's some epic sleep time, and it wouldn't break my heart one bit to reclaim it.

And it'd be nice to stop wrestling with these questions and just live my life. I mean, what difference does it really make if there is no heaven? That would mean there's also no hell. So, I'd live, die, and just…nothing. Not actually a big deal, now that I thought about it. Seemed like one really long night's sleep. No joy there, true. But no sadness or pain either. Could be way worse.

No more guilt, either. If there's no God, then I'm just a highly evolved animal. Why shouldn't I think about sex all the time? Why should't I watch whatever I darn well please?

I tried to force more and more thoughts like that. As the hours ticked by, I could almost make myself believe that God wasn't real. We'd imagined the whole thing, and I could go on living my life however I wanted.

But the nagging guilt wouldn't go away. If God wasn't real, then why the guilt? No one knew about the SD cards. No one would ever find out. Sim and I had done our work too well. But still, I was finding it harder and harder to make peace with myself after these sessions.

I couldn't reason God away. And the guilt weighed like a lead elephant on my chest.

When Tuesday morning dawned, it hit me. Jazz band was fourth period every Tuesday and Thursday. After that, the room was deserted, as was the entire school, for the rest of the afternoon. It was the perfect meeting space.

As I munched my way through a bowl of Fruit Loops, I shot a text off to Amy and Mark. *i think the jazz band room could be perfect. amy and i are in there 4th period TR but its open after that. should we meet today at 3?*

Moments later, Amy replied. *sounds great!*

Then Mark responded with, *Works for me! You guys mind if I bring Dani? We talked about this last night, and she's really interested, too.*

I wasn't sure what bothered me more. It was bad enough that the guy was now inviting other people to the first meeting of whatever this was, but who in his right mind bothers to be that grammatically precise in a text message?

It wasn't until I saw Sim in the hallway that I remembered we'd had plans to hang that afternoon. I begged out, but hesitated when it came to telling him why.

"Look, dude," he said. "I get it. You're a little twitterpated right now. It's fine. Just remember you do have a best friend who's going to want to hang out again eventually."

I nodded. I did feel bad about ignoring him for the past week. But he seemed to be taking it in stride, and I promised myself if this study thing turned out to be even remotely interesting, I'd loop him in on it.

As the rest of our pitiful band filed out of the jazz room at 2:50p, Amy started shifting a few of the more comfortable chairs into a haphazard circle. A few minutes later, Mark and Dani arrived.

It made a little more sense now. I hadn't known her name, but I'd seen Dani Miller with Mark around the school hallways enough to piece together that they were an item. I'd always thought them an odd pair. Mark was a little too proper about everything. He was the only guy in school that dressed like he wasn't a teenager. How many 18-year-old guys do you know that wear a tucked-in polo and slacks to class? You'd expect someone like that to date someone equally dorky, but Dani couldn't have seemed more different. Granted, I didn't know her at all, but when we'd shared classes she always seemed distant, almost rebellious. Whenever a teacher had called on her to answer a question, she answered with a tone that suggested she couldn't care less and had far better things to consider than algebra.

Forty-eight hours earlier I would have said I had nothing in common with these two. Yet here we were, gathered in the jazz band room of all places to try to answer history's greatest theological conundrums.

Yup, we're definitely crazy.

I introduced Amy to Dani, and everyone sat down. An awkward silence settled on the room before Mark finally asked, "So, how are we doing this?"

I'd spent a lot of time considering that very question since this appointment had been set the day before, and being the thoughtful, well-reasoned chap that I am, I crafted a thoughtful, well-reasoned plan.

"Let's just wing it," I said. "You guys don't really know us, and we don't really know you. Maybe for today we should just start there."

Mark nodded. "Sure. What do you want to know?"

"For starters, why did you guys want to do this?" I asked.

Mark turned to Dani. "You want to take this one?"

She shrugged. "Be my guest."

He cleared his throat. "Well, I've had questions on and off for a long time, but I guess the hard start for both of us would have to have been Mr. Weaver's Intro to Logic class last year. We weren't all that excited about it, but our parents thought it would help improve our college prospects."

"They got more than they bargained for," Dani chimed in.

Mark smiled. "Yeah. You see, during the course of the semester, Mr. Weaver taught us about a couple of logical rules that kinda wrecked things for Dani and me. The first was the law of non-contradiction. The law states that two or more contradictory ideas cannot both be true in the same sense at the same time. Basically, it's functionally impossible for me to be both here in this room and at home in my bedroom at the same time. From this, you can logically infer that if I'm here, then I'm not here. It's a weak example, but you get the point, yeah?"

Amy and I nodded. I had no idea where he was going with all this, but I was tracking with him so far.

"Dani and I agreed, reality follows this law. From everything we can observe, two contradictory ideas cannot both be true at the same time in the same way. If I say that Dani is a serial killer and a good person, then you must assume that I am mistaken about one of those two statements, or that I mean something different about one of them than it might appear. Maybe I mean she eats a huge breakfast rather than kills people."

"Different kinda cereal there genius," Dani said.

"You don't say?" Mark replied, sarcasm dripping. "Anyway, a serial killer cannot also be a good person at the same time that she's doing her serial killing. So both of my statements cannot be true. One can be true, or both could be false, but they cannot both be true."

"I'd agree with that," I said.

Amy nodded. "Seems pretty basic."

"Good," Mark said. "We're on the same page so far then. So, Dani and I started talking about this. If the law of non-contradiction is in fact real, then it must be real everywhere. If it's not, then it's not real. This next bit gets a little complicated, so stop me if I go too fast." He waited for a nod, then continued. "Our youth group at church had been doing a study on the attributes of God, and we'd spent a couple weeks talking about God's sovereignty. Our youth pastor kept hammering home the notion that the Bible says that God planned everything from the beginning, and everything has happened exactly as God decided things would happen. He's basically controlling everything. We read a quote by some guy, I guess a pretty well known Christian philosopher." He paused here and dug around in his backpack, finally retrieving a worn and crumpled page. "He said, 'To say that God foreordains all that comes to pass is simply to say that God is sovereign over his entire creation...If there is any part of creation outside of God's sovereignty, then God is simply not sovereign. If God is not sovereign, then God is not God.' The philosopher guy also said that where you fall on this question determines not just whether or not you're a Christian, but whether you're a theist or an atheist."

"Seriously?" I asked.

Mark nodded. "Yeah. Our youth pastor agreed with him. It was either believe that God predetermined everything or side with the atheists. But Dani and I had a hard time with it. There's so much evil and pain and suffering in the world. How could God, who the Bible says is good, predetermine that all that stuff would happen? Can someone who's good cause so much evil? We talked it to death in those weeks, then eventually life got busy and we forgot about it for a little while. But once Mr. Weaver started talking about the law of non-contradiction, we decided that if the law was true, then this particular 'sovereign' idea of God couldn't be."

He pulled a water bottle from his backpack and took a swig.

"I should explain what I mean by that because my parents misunderstood what I meant and…well, let's just say it didn't go well. They said, 'You can't submit God to your human understanding. You're finite and he's infinite. How could you hope to understand him?' On the surface, it seemed to make sense. We're fallible and limited. There's no way we can understand an infinite God. Except for one thing, as Dani pointed out to me later. The Infinite *made* it possible for us to understand him by revealing himself to us. We have the Bible. I can only assume that God gave us his Word so we could know about him. I believe this is confirmed by John 17." Mark pulled a Bible from his backpack and flipped through it. "Here we go. Verse 3 says, 'Now this is eternal life, that they know you, the only true God, and Jesus Christ, whom you have sent.' God intended for us to know him, and if an infinite being intended for the finite to know him, then I must conclude that he has given us the means by which we can do just that."

I was surprised as I listened to Mark tell his story. I'd always thought he was just a dork who took himself way too seriously. Tall, and thin to the point of looking unhealthy, his appearance just screamed "awkward." But up close, hearing him talk about logic and the finite and the infinite…it was kind of inspiring.

"Seems like you've spent a little time on this," Amy said.

Mark grinned. "You have no idea. Dani and I spent weeks debating this point, arguing back and forth trying to decide, can we actually understand God? Most people would say we can know him, but that truly understanding God is impossible. I get where they're coming from. I freely admit, I can't wrap my head around an infinite existence. But we have to be able to understand some things about God, or else what's the point? So, we started asking which things about God could we understand. Ultimately, we decided that since we're finite, we can only understand the things God himself has revealed to us, either through creation or through his Word. And he must have given us a means of understanding his Word. That's where logic comes in.

"The bottom line is this: we have to be able to apply logic and reason to the entirety of the Bible. If we say at any point that 'You can't use reason there,' then we lose the right to apply reason to any of the rest of it. You're left with anarchy, and again, what's the point?"

Amy nodded. "So you concluded that if anything the Bible said could be understood with reason, then the whole thing must be understandable. And if something it said seemed to conflict with the basic rules of reality…"

"…Then there was a better than even chance that we were misunderstanding what it said." Mark finished. "That's exactly it. Like I said, it's complicated, but we seem to be tracking together so far, yeah?"

We nodded, though in truth I felt like I was barely keeping up.

"Now, there needs to be a starting point, a foundation from which we can reason that will keep us grounded. Obviously, that should be the Bible. It's God's revealed Word, so we start there."

"And?" I asked. "What have you found?"

"Nothing yet," Dani said. "We reached that point in our thoughts on it just last week. When Mark overheard you guys in the cafeteria yesterday, he figured if other people are asking similar questions, why not join forces?"

"I guess that makes sense," I said, admitting to myself that maybe having Mark and Dani involved in this wasn't going to be such a bad thing after all. "If you were to boil it down then, what would you say your primary question is?"

Mark thought a minute. "Well, the Bible refers to God as 'sovereign' all over the place. There's no question that he is. Our question then would have to be, what does that mean? Does it really mean that he predetermined everything? And if so, how do we reckon with that?"

It was getting creepy how similar their questions sounded to my own. I'd been wondering for weeks what I was going to do with God if it turned out that he actually had planned everything to happen this way.

I pulled a notebook and pen from my backpack and flipped to a fresh page.

"How does this sound?" I asked. "We'll call it question one: if God is good and sovereign, then how can evil exist? If God causes evil, can he be truly good?"

"Sounds about right," Mark said.

"What about you guys?" Dani asked. "What's your story?"

I looked at Amy, and she nodded back at me. "Well, the biggest question on my mind right now has to do with election," I said. "You guys know what I mean, right?"

"Yup," Dani said. "You're referring to whether or not God chooses who get's saved, right?"

I nodded. "My pastor gave a sermon a month ago about God's sovereignty, specifically in regard to who gets saved and who doesn't. He said we just have to accept that God chooses who gets saved and who goes to hell, and that it doesn't conflict with his love or goodness. I've had a hard time making peace with that."

"Can't imagine why," Dani quipped.

Mark nodded. "Kind of an extension of question one. How does election work? Do we choose our eternal destinies, or does God choose for us?"

I wrote it down on a second line. It felt different enough to warrant its own space.

"What about you, Amy?" Mark asked.

After a silent moment, Amy shook her head. "Nothing to add at the moment. These sound like great questions to start with."

I read the two questions again, silently. "We've only got

two questions here, but I don't think they're going to be easy. Should we split up the questions?"

Dani shook her head. "I don't think so. We should all study each of the questions. It'll increase our chances of really understanding what the Bible is saying about each of them. We'll be able to challenge each other."

I could see immediately that she was right. "Okay then, should we all just focus on question one this week, and we'll meet again next Tuesday?"

Everyone nodded, but Dani added, "I think we should set some ground rules before we leave."

"What'd you have in mind?" Amy asked.

Dani leaned forward. "The very first thing that comes to mind is that we shouldn't tell anyone what we're doing. Mark and I both had bad experiences when we tried to talk to our parents about these questions, and our youth pastor at First Baptist wasn't any more receptive."

I imagined telling Dad about all this.

"Yeah, I'd say that's probably a good idea."

"What if we hear someone asking questions like these?" Amy asked. "Like Mark heard us in the cafeteria. If they're already asking these questions, it would probably be safer then."

"Fair enough," Dani granted. "Tell no one what we're doing unless you hear them asking these kinds of questions for themselves already."

I scribbled it down just so we'd have a record. "Okay, what else?"

"I don't think we should keep any questions to ourselves," Mark said. "If we have questions, it's a reasonable assumption that we're not the only ones, and that makes them fair game. If Christianity fails to stand up to even a single challenge, then it's not true. And if it is true, then it has nothing to fear from even the toughest scrutiny."

"*No...question...can...remain...unasked,*" I echoed as I wrote. "Anything else?"

"I don't think we should fake acceptance," Dani said. "If something doesn't sit right with someone, it may be because it isn't right. That might be dangerous because we're obviously fallible, and our hearts may not like the truth. But leaving something like that to fester could poison our entire perception of God. We should push through until our biblical understanding is satisfying for everyone."

More scribbling. "That it?"

"I think everyone should be required to study every question, " Amy said. "We're talking about the nature of reality and eternity here. I don't see how anything could be more important. If we're going to do this, we should commit here and now to making the time for it."

I nodded, and penned in the fourth rule.

"Here's what we have, then," I said. "Rule one, tell no one what we're doing unless we hear them asking similar questions on their own first. Rule two, no question can remain unasked. Rule three, never fake acceptance. Rule four, everyone makes the time to study each question each week."

"Sounds about right," Amy said. Mark nodded. Dani was lost in something on her phone.

"Well, I guess we have our homework for next Tuesday." I paused not wanting to ask the question that kept gnawing at the back of my mind. But, rule two…

"What if…" I began, uncertain. "What if all this leads us to conclude that God doesn't exist? Do we just walk away?"

Dani clicked her phone off and looked at me. "In direct answer to your question, if the facts lead to a universe without God, then yes, we'd have to allow for that. But I know He exists. So do you. I could spout all kinds of 'proofs' at you." She threw up fingered quotation marks as she said this. "I could go on and on about the fundamental need for a first cause. I could talk about the second law of thermodynamics and how everything is moving to a state of entropy, so things don't get better and more complex as evolution would have us believe. I *could* do that. But I don't have to. The very fact that you're sitting in this room tells me you've already failed to convince yourself that God doesn't exist. Something in you won't allow you to let go because deep down you know it's true. You may not know what to do about it yet, but you know he's real. And you know you're going to have to reckon with that."

I felt frozen to my seat. I couldn't move, and I couldn't look away from her. She'd pegged me, and I suddenly felt like I was sitting stark naked in front of everyone.

Mark chuckled. "There's my Dani, blunt as a hammer. She gets the point across, though, doesn't she?"

9

Amy and I were both pretty quiet as we walked toward Otis. I kept playing the whole thing over in my head. Dani was exactly right. I couldn't reason God away. He was real, and whatever that meant, I had to deal with it. It would likely prove the most important question of my life, and I needed an answer.

Reaching the lot, we said goodbye to Mark and Dani. Weird to think I'd see them in school the next day. Weirder still to think I'd feel closer to them than most people at school, and we'd only just gotten to know each other.

I opened Amy's door for her, then circled Otis and slid into my own seat. I buckled in and sighed.

"Well, that was different," Amy said.

I chuckled. "No kidding. I'm still trying to convince myself that it actually happened and that I'm not dreaming."

I felt a sharp pain in my arm and cried out. Amy laughed.

"You pinched me?"

"Yes, I did. Now you can stop trying to convince yourself. You're clearly awake."

I shook my head. "Okay, next time I say that, let's just assume that I'm speaking poetically, all right?"

Amy feigned disappointment. "Oh, but it's so much more fun to take you literally."

I smiled. "So, what do you think?"

Amy shrugged and shook her head. "I can't think of a single thing they said that I disagree with. I'm just shocked to find there are actually others in school feeling the same way."

I nodded, my eyes fixed on the road. "I know what you mean."

"Dani said they go to First Baptist. Have you ever been there?"

I nodded. "Yeah, there was a big lock-in a couple years back. A bunch of youth groups in the area. First Baptist hosted since they have the largest and nicest facilities for that kind of thing."

Amy shook her head. "One of the biggest churches in town, and they have at least two kids asking questions they don't feel free to bring up in church. That's just wrong."

I didn't say anything. I agreed, of course, but I couldn't think of anything to say that we hadn't already said. Most adults didn't seem to understand the questions we were asking or why we needed to know so badly. But I had a gnawing in my gut that I hadn't *really* given my parents a chance to answer the questions yet. True, Dad hadn't responded well to any kind of doubt in the past, but this wasn't really doubt. I wasn't questioning God. I was just questioning if what we believed about God was accurate. That couldn't be out of line.

Could it?

I dropped Amy off at home, jealously relinquishing her hand as she slid from my passenger seat. It was getting harder and harder to let her leave. I wanted to be with her every second.

I pulled into my own driveway just before four.

"Hello?" I heard from the dining room as soon as I stepped in the house. "Nathan, is that you?"

"Yeah, Mom, I'm home."

She stuck her head around the corner looking worried. "You're later than I expected. Everything okay?"

I silently cursed myself for not updating them. Mom and Dad didn't normally follow up on a my movements, as long as they believed they already knew where I was.

"Sorry," I said, scrambling. "I had a late study group after jazz band."

"Oh, okay," she said, evidently satisfied. "What class was it for?"

"It's for Bible," I said, trying to convince myself that I wasn't exactly lying.

"All right. Well, dinner's at seven," she said, turning back to whatever she'd been doing before I walked in.

I tried to avoid running for my room. My heart was racing, despite my efforts to control my breathing. I didn't like being dishonest with Mom. Even if it wasn't an outright lie, I knew I wasn't being truthful. And when we sat down to a dinner of hot dogs and macaroni and cheese, I decided it was as good a time as any to see what she and Dad thought about my questions.

My mouth half-full of my second bite of hot dog, I asked, "So, I've been wondering a bit about one of Pastor B's recent sermons."

"The one on tithing?" Dad asked.

I swallowed the hot dog, and shook my head. "Uh-uh. A few weeks before that, about election and predestination and all that."

"Oh yeah?" Dad sounded interested.

"Yeah. I guess I've just been wondering if you and Mom agree with him. Do you think God really chose who would get saved and who wouldn't before he created anyone?"

"Sure we do," Dad said. Not even a moment's hesitation. "The Bible makes it pretty clear. God chose us from 'before the foundation of the world.' Says so right there in the first chapter of Ephesians. We can look it up after dinner, but it's hard to come to any other conclusion based on the Scripture."

I thought about what Mark had said. *If Christianity fails to stand up to even a single challenge, then it's not true. And if it is true, then it has nothing to fear from even the toughest questions.* I took a breath and pressed on.

"I understand that's what the verse *seems* to say," I said, trying to pick my words with as much care as possible. "But doesn't that seem harsh? I mean, before people have even done anything wrong, God decides that they're going to go to hell? That would mean that most people are going to hell without even having a chance to choose otherwise."

Dad's face darkened. "Be careful, Nathan. It's a dangerous thing to start deciding what God can and can't do. You start putting yourself in his place, and you make the same mistake Lucifer did."

Wow. Sixty whole seconds into the conversation, and Dad's already comparing me to Satan. Awesome.

"It's just a question, Dad. What are you afraid of?"

"I'm not afraid of anything, Nathan. And you will watch your tone, do you understand? God created the world, and he made it in the way that seemed best to him. It's not for us to question how he chose to do it, but to simply believe and worship him for who he is. Can you do that or not?"

The honest answer was, of course, no. I couldn't *just* believe without investigating this further. If it turned out that I had to believe this in order to be a Christian, then I'd deal with that when the time came. But there was a lot of digging yet to do before I'd concede that necessity.

"Well, yeah, I guess so," I lied. I hated that it was necessary, but what else was I supposed to do? Declare my allegiance with the devil at the dinner table?

"Good," Dad said. He seemed satisfied for the moment. "I'm glad you have questions about Pastor Bennington's teaching, but you have to be careful to not put yourself in God's place. All kinds of error starts there."

I nodded, but I wasn't listening anymore. I picked at my hot dog and macaroni, but my appetite had vanished along with any hope of talking about these things with Dad. I might try with Mom alone later, if for no other reason than to know that I'd tried. But it seemed for now that Amy, Mark, and Dani were the people with whom I could safely ask the questions that wouldn't go away.

❖　　❖　　❖

When I woke up that Wednesday morning, I was still pretty irked at Dad. I'd planned to grab a bowl of cereal before school, but when I found him at the kitchen table with his coffee and Bible, I opted for a pack of Pop-Tarts instead. I couldn't stomach trying to make small talk.

As I munched the pastries on the patio, another problem presented itself. I'd told myself that if the study group turned out to be interesting, I would fill Sim in. But I had also just committed to the group, including Amy, that I wouldn't tell anyone about it. At least, not until they had voiced their own questions about God. Compounding the problem was that I would have to tell Sim something about the previous night. The moron was gonna ask, and I played it coy he'd start making up his own theories. Blowing him off was not an option.

His car came around the corner, and I decided there was only one option. I had to find out if Sim was harboring any questions of his own.

"So, how'd it go?" he asked, barely letting me open the door before opening his mouth.

I rolled my eyes. "Good morning to you, too."

"Yeah, yeah, good morning. Whatever." Sim put the car in reverse and started backing out of the drive. "Come on now. I was stuck with nothing but homework all evening. Throw your best friend a bone here."

"Appropriate that you would compare yourself to a dog. Maybe I should get you a shock collar. I might finally get some peace and quiet."

"Agghh!" Sim cried, throwing his hands up before slapping them back down on the wheel. "You're impossible."

I chuckled. "Relax, dude. You know getting worked up only makes you an easier target. Besides, the afternoon was pretty quiet. We studied together for a while, and then I took her home. "

Sim yawned, a gaping yawn that started real enough only to be exaggerated in mockery. He shook his head. "Only you could manage to spend an afternoon with a girl like that and have it turn out boring."

I punched his arm. "Whatever, man. Just drive the car."

Sim smiled, clearly more comfortable dishing the trash than taking it. "So, what? Did you guys at least talk about anything interesting?"

I shrugged. "I guess so. We talked about her dad a bit. He worked for the Coast Guard before dying in the line of duty."

"Dude, that sucks."

I sensed an opening. "I know. It's created some pretty big questions for her when it comes to God. You know, 'how could a good God let something like that happen' and all that."

"Hm."

Hm? That's it? I'd expected a bigger reaction.

I pressed harder. "I can't imagine trying to come to terms with something like that. Can you?"

He didn't answer at first. After a few seconds, I began to wonder if he was going to respond at all. Finally, he said, "I don't know, man. Stuff like that, it just kinda makes the whole thing seem a little iffy. You know?"

"Iffy? What do you mean?"

"Ahh, I don't really wanna get in to it. I know you believe, and that's cool."

I was having trouble processing what I was hearing. Sim and I rarely talked about anything having to do with God. I knew his family went to church, though a different one than we did. But between that and the fact that we'd both attended Knight's Day since sixth grade, I guess I just assumed that we were pretty much on the same page when it came to Christianity.

"Are you saying you don't believe in God?" I asked.

Sim sighed, clearly uncomfortable with this turn in the conversation. "Maybe. I don't know. I just have a hard time with the whole thing. I mean, evolution seems like a bit of a stretch, but I can't say that the Bible seems to make any more sense. I just have a hard time with the whole thing."

"So, you're not a Christian?"

He fell silent again, then slowly shook his head. "I don't think so."

"Wow." I hadn't been prepared for this at all. "So, you're what? An atheist?"

"Maybe. Probably more of an agnostic. I honestly just don't know. And I don't know that I ever will. Doesn't seem like anyone's been able to present a convincing case either way. I don't really expect that to change."

I couldn't believe it. We'd been best friends for more than a decade. How had I missed this?

"We gonna be okay?" Sim asked.

I looked at him. "Yeah, man. Of course, we are. I'm just

a little surprised."

"Really? I thought you'd figured it out by now. It's not like I've ever talked much about God."

I shook my head. "I guess I just always assumed we were on the same page so there wasn't much reason to. I'm sorry, dude. I should have asked you about it sooner."

"It's really not a big a deal," he said in a way that almost made me believe it. "I'm still the same guy. Bottom line is, I just don't think about this kind of thing all that much."

I didn't respond. I couldn't fathom the question not mattering. And now I couldn't tell him what I'd really been doing the previous afternoon.

I felt like crap hiding it from him.

I told Amy about Sim during free period. She obviously hadn't known him as long as I had, so the news didn't seem to come as much of a shock to her. But she could tell what it meant to me.

I was pretty quiet for most of the period. To fill the time, I copied the questions from our meeting so everyone could have them for reference as we moved forward. It came out like this:

The List

1. If God is good and sovereign, then how can evil exist? If He causes evil, can He truly be good?

2. How does election work? Can people choose their eternal destiny, or does God choose for them?

The Rules

1. Tell no one what we're doing unless we hear them asking similar questions on their own first.

2. No question can remain unasked.

3. Never fake acceptance.

4. Everyone must make the time to study each question each week.

Amy laughed when I handed her a copy. "Not much of a list, is it?"

I cracked a grin. "I guess I'm expecting it to grow."

"We'll have to make some time for our new homework."

Homework. Ugh...

I thought about the assignments that were starting to pile up for my other classes.

I folded up the paper and slid it into my backpack. "I understand we have to make time for this, but it's not gonna be easy with mid-terms coming up."

"It does seem like a lot. How about this? We have enough classes together. Why don't you come over to my house on Saturday? You have worship practice that morning, right?"

I nodded.

"So, come by after. You can tell your parents that we're helping each other get ready for midterms. Which is the truth. We'll definitely work on that. But we can also take a little time to start working on question one."

If I had to spend an entire Saturday studying, having Amy there would make it about a million times more tolerable.

"Sounds good," I said. "But just in case it comes up

when my dad's around, let's say that Sim'll be there. We can always invite him over later in the afternoon so it'll be true."

"What's wrong?"

I shook my head. "Suffice it to say Dad's convinced that I'm not emotionally mature enough to handle a relationship with a member of the opposite sex. He wasn't thrilled that we went into Denver together on Saturday."

"You think you'll get in trouble if he finds out?"

"Maybe. Maybe, but I tried talking to him about the election question last night, and he wasn't exactly open to a dissenting opinion. If he can't engage with me on these things, then I'm gonna have a hard time caring what he thinks about who I spend my time with."

Amy hesitated. It was clear I'd made her uncomfortable talking about Dad like that.

"I'm sorry," she said after a moment. "I guess I thought you got along pretty well with your parents."

"Mom's fine," I allowed. "She at least listens. But in the end, she generally sides with Dad. And Dad… I don't know. Seems like we've been avoiding each other for years. He's always had a short temper, and he cheated on Mom when I was twelve. I've had a hard time relating to him ever since. And now, when I try to ask a simple question, he makes it this huge thing as though I'm questioning God just like Satan did."

"Seriously?"

I nodded. "We weren't two full minutes into the conversation when he dropped that bomb. Pretty much killed any further discussion."

She took my hand, but didn't say anything.

"Anyway," I said, trying to not sound as frustrated as I felt. "I'd prefer to just stay out of his way right now."

10

Over the next few days, I managed to do a decent job staying on Dad's good side. I was diligent with homework, kept dinner conversation light, and generally avoided all mention of anything pertaining to theology or Amy.

Because that's how it's supposed to be, right? You're supposed to talk to your parents about everything except what really matters to you.

Things were awkward with Sim, too. We'd never spent much time talking about God before, and it had never mattered. But now that we'd cracked that door open, it seemed impossible to close. When we drove to school together we shot the breeze just like we always had. But now it seemed like we were avoiding something. Because, of course, we were. By Friday, I was driving myself to school, just to avoid the awkward fifteen minutes of, again, talking about everything except what I really wanted to talk about.

In the space of a month, my life had changed completely. Whatever had been important before the school year didn't even appear on the radar now.

Now I had my questions, and I had Amy.

That Saturday, I raced to her house after worship practice, once again struck at the strangeness of practicing worship. God forbid anything spontaneous ever happen in church.

We spent a couple hours working on algebra and church history. AmLit was cake thanks to Amy's perspective on *Gatsby.* The paper practically wrote itself.

After lunch, Mrs. Davidson announced she was going to take a nap. With her mom safely unconscious, Amy and I turned our attention to The List.

"Question one," she read in a hushed tone. "If God is good and sovereign, then how can evil exist? If He causes evil, can He truly be good?"

We were both silent for a minute as we pondered the question. The situation was absurd. Here we were, two seventeen-year-olds, and in the space of a Saturday afternoon we were going to solve one of Christianity's most enduring mysteries. Next up, world hunger!

Amy spoke first. "Maybe we should break it down a bit."

I nodded. "Okay."

She opened a notebook to a fresh page. "Let's start with 'sovereign.' What do we mean by that?"

"Well, when Pastor B was talking about sovereignty, he seemed to think that God determined and controlled everything that happened. I would assume that's the definition we're working with here."

Amy rewrote the question.

"So, if God is good and determines and controls everything that happens, then how can evil exist?"

I chewed my bottom lip. "Well, the Bible says God is good, right?"

Amy opened a web browser on her Mom's laptop and ran a search. "Yup, confirmed. Multiple Psalms recognize God as good. And Jesus said that there was only one who was good. The Father."

"Okay, then we know God is good, and we know that evil exists. So it's not really a question of 'if.' God *is* good, and evil *does* exist. What was that logic rule Mark was talking about?"

"The law of non-contradiction."

"Right," I said, glad her memory was better than mine. "So, we know that I can't be both good and a murderer. Good people can't be evil without ceasing to be good. So, if God is good all the time, then he couldn't cause evil."

Amy nodded. "Makes sense. There's that parable, too. About the tree."

"Which one?" I asked. "Aren't there several?"

She returned to the computer. A minute or two later she said, "Here it is. Matthew 7:17-20, 'Likewise, every good tree bears good fruit, but a bad tree bears bad fruit. A good tree cannot bear bad fruit, and a bad tree cannot bear good fruit. Every tree that does not bear good fruit is cut down and thrown into the fire. Thus, by their fruit you will recognize them.'"

"Who's them?"

She scanned back up. "Based on verse 15, the whole passage is talking about watching out for false prophets. But wouldn't you think that this kind of litmus test would have to apply to everyone. Men, women, prophets, preachers, angels…God himself? We know them by their fruit. I mean, God even tells us what his fruit is!"

"You're right," I said. "It's in Ephesians, isn't it?"

"Galatians, I think." Another search. "Yup, Galatians 5:22-23, 'The fruit of the Spirit is love, joy, peace, forbearance, kindness, goodness, faithfulness, gentleness, and self-control. Against such things there is no law.'"

I swallowed my embarrassment at how much better she seemed to now the Bible than I did. "The Holy Spirit is God, right? So, we could just as well say the fruit of God is love, joy, et cetera, et cetera. Right?"

"Yup," Amy agreed.

"Okay," I pressed on. "And it seems pretty obvious that these are good fruits, which by God's own definition means he's a good tree. Because a bad tree can't bear good fruit. But as a good tree, that would also mean that God can't bear bad fruit."

"Yup," Amy said again. "I'm with you. Keep going."

"So, this would suggest that God, as a good tree, cannot be the source of evil. It would be the very definition of bad fruit. And yet, we know that there is bad fruit in the world. Murder, rape, theft, adultery, war…it's all over the place. And now we have both logic and the Bible itself indicating that God is a good tree who cannot bear bad fruit, yet there is undeniably bad fruit in the world."

"Which then begs the question," Amy said, pausing for effect. "If it's not God, then what or who is the source of the bad fruit? And if there's another source, then it would mean that God isn't determining and causing everything after all."

"Then who's the source?"

"Satan, maybe? Probably all of the angels and people that have ever followed him, too."

"Could be. Genesis does say that when God was finished with creation, it was all very good. Then we strolled in and messed up his very good world."

Amy grimaced.

"What's wrong?" I asked.

She shook her head. "I'm not sure. I mean, that makes sense. But does the Bible fully back it up? I mean, isn't God supposed to be all-powerful or omnipotent or whatever?"

I shrugged and nodded toward the computer. "Let's check."

"Thank God for Google," she said, running the new search.

"No kidding," I agreed. "Can you imagine doing this with just a concordance?"

She nodded, scrolling through a page of results. "Nothing in the NIV about omnipotent. Let me try something else." She ran another search. "Here we go. Revelation 19:6 in the KJV. 'The Lord God omnipotent reigneth.' The NIV has the same verse down as, 'The Lord our God the Almighty reigns.' So, God is omnipotent, but logic and the Bible both indicate that evil things are happening that he doesn't cause. How is that possible?"

I sighed. "Ten minutes into this thing and my head is already starting to hurt."

Amy laughed. "I imagine that's a standard problem when trying to understand the infinite."

"I'm gonna need to buy stock in Tylenol."

She nodded toward the kitchen. "Cabinet above the sink."

I went to get the painkillers and a glass of water. Returning to the table, I asked, "How are we defining omnipotent?"

Another search.

"We have a few definitions here. Almighty or infinite in power. Having very great or unlimited authority or power. Having unlimited power, able to do anything."

"Huh. So the definition doesn't have to mean that God causes everything. Just that he has the power to do anything he chooses. That he's 'able to do anything,' right?"

Amy nodded. "That sounds about right. And it makes sense. He is God, after all. He created everything. He'd have to have infinite power to do that. But it doesn't necessarily mean that no one *else* could have any power. They wouldn't have as much power as God, and if they tried to stand up to Him, like Satan, God would win every time. But if God didn't stop someone, they would be able to do anything their limited power allowed."

I thought about it. "Something like reach up and pluck a piece of fruit from a forbidden tree?"

"I think so," she said.

"It would definitely help make sense of passages like when Joshua tells Israel to choose for themselves who they would serve. Or when God tells Israel to choose life that they might live. Both of those are pretty meaningless statements if people don't actually have the power to choose."

"Let's try something else," Amy said, entering a search for "Almighty".

We spent the next hour going through reference after reference to God being Almighty, and to more references to people making *choices* for or against God, for righteousness or for evil. There were passages about God sustaining the world, but nothing directly stating that he tyrannically controlled every single event. In numerous places, he put a choice before people and held them accountable for what *they* chose.

When we finally leaned back, our eyes tired from the strain of staring at the screen for so long, Amy sighed. "It kinda seems too easy, doesn't it?"

"What do you mean?"

"I mean, people have been arguing about sovereignty and free will forever. We just came to a conclusion in an hour and a half. You think we're missing something?"

I thought about it. "It's possible, but I got nothing."

Amy closed the laptop. "Well, it's a decent start anyway."

By Tuesday afternoon, I was ready to sleep for the rest of the week. Every spare minute had been spent prepping for midterms. Monday brought the agony of Algebra II and the sheer torture of a fitness exam that included running lines in the gym. I felt okay about the algebra exam, but the run was enough to make me think about joining Sim at Ringling Bros.

Tuesday was Church History and an essay on the immediate effects of Luther's Theses on the Catholic church. They've written who knows how much on that topic, and I was supposed to sum it up in 500 words. Wasn't exactly comprehensive.

Amy and I commiserated about the exams we'd finished and the ones still to come as we walked into the Jazz Band room.

Dani was already there. We said "Hi," then settled in to an awkward silence. Dani tapped away at her phone.

Mark showed up at 3:05. "Is this week over yet?" he asked, collapsing into a chair.

We responded with a collective grunt. No one wanted to dwell on the rest of the week.

"You guys find time to start working through the List?" He asked.

I pulled out my notes from Saturday and filled them in on the conclusions Amy and I had reached. Our definitions of sovereign and omnipotent, and our conclusions about God having infinite power, but other people having power, too, as long as God didn't choose to act against them.

As I wrapped up, I tried to read Mark's face, but he didn't give away much. I wondered if they'd come to a different answer than what we'd found.

"Huh," was all he gave me.

"'Huh?'" I echoed. "That's it?"

"It's just weird."

"What's weird? You guys find something different?"

"Actually, no," he said. "That's almost the exact conclusion we came to. Down to the verse."

Amy cleared her throat. "Doesn't it seem odd that this answer seems to fly in the face of what all of our parents and pastors and churches believe? I mean, are we missing something here?"

"We wondered that when we finished our study," Dani said, finally looking up from her phone. "So I did some checking. Turns out there are a lot of people out there that think this way."

I leaned forward. "How many is a lot?"

"Statistics indicate that it may be a 50-50 split," Dani said. "There's not a lot of great information on this. It most often gets couched in the terminology of the Calvinism vs. Arminianism debate. But the truth seems to be that a whole lot of people that call themselves Christians don't really know what they believe about this question, and among those that do know, it's a pretty even split."

I shook my head. "How is it possible that I didn't know that?"

Mark shrugged, then Dani said, "Think about it. How long have you really been asking these questions?"

I paused. She was right. I hadn't ever stopped to consider this stuff until very recently.

"I guess not all that long," I admitted. "Still, my pastor and my parents all act like this is the only possible thing you can believe about God's sovereignty."

"Yeah, mine too," Dani said. "God knows why, but they don't handle disagreement about this very well. It's their way or the highway."

"Which is sad," Mark cut in. "Don't get me wrong. This is an important question, and it impacts countless other doctrines. But in the end, I don't think anyone's getting saved because they have a right opinion about how God's power works. At worst, someone might be prevented from coming to God because they can't accept the answer they've been given. If more Christians acknowledged that there was more than one school of thought on this issue, I think it'd make it easier for a lot of people to accept the basic concept that God exists."

"So, what?" I asked. "We'll have an answer we like, and they'll have an answer they like, and that'll be it? Truth'll be whatever you want it to be?"

Mark shook his head. "No, that's not what I meant at all. It'd violate the law of non-contradiction. They can be right, or we can be right, or we both can be wrong. But two contradictory ideas like this can't both be true. I think my point is more that the Bible doesn't say anything about having to believe the right things about how God's power works in order to be saved. It doesn't make a wrong belief right, or even safe, but it does mean that having a wrong idea about this doctrine isn't necessarily a fatal flaw."

I thought about that. For all his faults, Dad seemed sincere in his faith. Most mornings he had his Bible at the breakfast table, and he'd been really involved at church since forever. There was something reassuring about the idea that we might be able to disagree about this and yet still find some kind of common ground.

All the same, I wasn't in a hurry to raise the conversation with him again.

"Did you get a chance to look at the election question?" Mark asked, interrupting my thoughts.

"Not really," Amy said. "Midterms kinda crowded out our time."

Mark gave a sympathetic nod.

"What about you guys?" I asked.

"We did look at it, and made some good progress, I think," Mark said. "I guess we can proceed one of two ways. If you want to start looking at it for yourselves free of any bias from us, we can wait and talk about it next week. If you don't care, we can share some of our thoughts."

Amy and I looked at each other. She nodded. I shrugged. "Go ahead," I said. "I don't have much experience with this topic yet. A sermon my pastor gave a few weeks back was the first time I've ever given it much thought."

"What'd your pastor have to say?" Mark asked.

"He came down on the side of God choosing everyone's eternal destiny before Creation. He quoted some verse from Ephesians. I can't remember where exactly."

Dani tapped away at her phone. After a moment, she asked, "Is this it? 'For he chose us in him before the creation of the world to be holy and blameless in his sight. In love he predestined us for adoption to sonship through Jesus Christ, in accordance with his pleasure and will— to the praise of his glorious grace, which he has freely given us in the One he loves.'"

I nodded. "Yup, that's the one."

"Ephesians 1:4-6," she said.

"And what were your thoughts?" Mark prodded.

I thought back to sitting on the roof after church. "It made me question whether I wanted anything to do with God. As Pastor B pointed out, if God chose those that would be saved, then He also chose those that wouldn't. I couldn't believe that God would condemn someone that hadn't even been born yet."

"Even if that's what the Bible says?" Dani challenged.

I hadn't expected that. I thought they were going to tell us why they disagreed with this position, not try to convince us that we should believe it.

"I don't know," I said. "I wouldn't want to believe it. I don't know that I could love a God that did that. I guess if that is what the Bible says...I don't know. Are you saying this is the conclusion you came to?"

"Didn't say that," Dani said. "Just wanted to see what you'd say."

Mark leaned forward. "There are a number of passages that make it seem that God chose the saved and the unsaved before creation. Dani, let's take that passage apart a bit. Read the first part again."

Dani cleared her throat. "'For he chose us in him before the creation of the world...'"

"Okay, stop there," Mark interrupted. "'For he chose us in him...' Who's *us*?"

I thought for a moment.

"Christians, I guess," Amy answered.

"Exactly," Mark said. "Now Dani, read the first verse of the chapter."

"'Paul, an apostle of Christ Jesus by the will of God, to God's holy people in Ephesus, the faithful in Christ Jesus...'"

Mark nodded. "So, Christians." He pulled his own Bible out of the backpack by his chair and flipped through it. "For he chose us, Christians, *in him*... that's the next part, and we think it's key. God didn't just choose us before the creation of the world. He chose us in *him*, and the context indicates that *him* is Christ. God chose Christians in Christ before the creation of the world."

"Okay…" I said, still not really sure how this knowledge changed what the passage was saying.

"There's another verse in Revelation that played into it." Mark flipped to the back of his Bible. "13:8. 'All inhabitants of the earth will worship the beast—all whose names have not been written in the Lamb's book of life, the Lamb who was slain from the creation of the world.' The passage is talking about the end times and the Beast, and most of that doesn't really have anything to do with what we're talking about now. It's that last part of the verse. '…the Lamb who was slain from the creation of the world.' God had that plan in place from the beginning. He knew that sin would enter the equation at some point, and he set a plan in place for our redemption. He chose from 'before the creation of the world' to send Christ."

My head was starting to hurt again.

Amy nodded. "So, when God chose from the start to send Jesus, he also chose to save anyone that would one day believe in Christ."

"That's it," Mark said. "That's what we think about election. God couldn't have damned anyone without them first choosing against him. To do so would violate the law of non-contradiction. He couldn't be good while at the same time condemning innocents. And if he's choosing for us, it renders meaningless all of those places that he commands people to choose for or against him. A plain reading of the *entire* passage in Ephesians makes it clear that everyone still has a choice. God has had this plan since the beginning, but people make their choices for or against him every day. And it's those choices that ultimately decide a person's eternal destiny. Make sense?"

I nodded, mostly getting it. I was going to have to dig into it some more later, but what he said seemed to add up.

As if reading my mind, Mark said, "You should absolutely look at it more for yourselves. There were plenty of other verses that deal with this topic, and you should read all of them to get the full picture." He handed me a list.

I took it, curious, though I suspected it was going to have to wait until after midterms were over.

We spent the rest of the afternoon talking about the questions. Amy threw out some more challenges about other verses that affected questions 1 and 2. I listened, but only sort of. It was possible now that God wasn't a sadistic tyrant, and that was good.

But good or not, I still wasn't sure what to do with him.

11

Why does so much of history have to be boring?

I can't imagine the events were actually boring when they happened. The Roman Empire must reek of fascinating anecdotes. The period surrounding the American and French Revolutions reshaped western civilization. Gotta be some compelling stuff there. Even the dark ages had the Crusades, the bubonic plague, and a war that lasted a solid century. These had to be epic events full of great stories.

But when it comes to actually conveying the history, it seems there's an unspoken rule among history writers that they make their works as mind-numbingly boring as possible.

I guess I can't speak for every history book, as I haven't read that many. Maybe the powers that be at Knight's Day pick the boring books on purpose. Maybe they're just sadists. It's a possibility I've never ruled out.

Given the inspiring way Ms. Waller had presented our final project for Bible class, I'd hoped she might know of some good material on John Wesley.

No dice.

Friday evening following the theological rebel group, round 2, found me sitting on my bed surrounded by a blank notebook and three books on John Wesley and the history of the Methodist movement. I opened the first one, inventively titled, *The Life of John Wesley:*

> *"The sect, or Society, as they would call themselves, of Methodists, has existed for the greater part of the century: they have their seminaries and their hierarchy, their own regulations, their own manners, their own literature: in England they form a distinct people, an imperium in imperio: they are extending widely in America; and in both countries they number their annual increase by thousands..."*

Oh God, kill me now.

I closed the book and threw it to the foot of the bed. It was October 16th. And it was a Friday night. I still had almost two months until the project was due. I'm not normally a procrastinator, but with the rest of the reading promising to be as bland as the first paragraph, Mr. Wesley seemed to warrant an exception.

I stood up and stretched. Amy was spending the night with her mom, and I didn't really feel like hanging out with anyone else. Things had settled down a bit with Sim, but we still needed time.

I grabbed my backpack from the dresser and pulled out *The List*. It annoyed me. The whole thing seemed way too easy. If these questions could be answered so quickly, and apparently with the Bible backing up those answers, then why in the world didn't everyone believe this? Why would anyone choose to believe something that A) made God look terrible, and B) flies in the face of any kind of sense?

It just wouldn't reconcile. I'd tried since Tuesday night to get excited about finally having answers, but the answers just raised more questions. Why couldn't Pastor B see the truth if it was so simple? Why couldn't Dad? Why did asking questions about this cause Dad to respond so antagonistically?

And why didn't I feel any closer to understanding God or what he wanted from me?

I'd been a Christian for almost as long as I could remember. When I was five, Dad led me through the Sinner's Prayer. Looking back on it now, I'm not sure I fully understood what I was doing. But I believed it then, and I guess I still believe it now. I believe that Jesus lived, died for my sins, and rose again. And I'd heard time and again that if I confess with my mouth that Jesus is Lord and believe in my heart that he was raised from the dead, then I'd be saved.

Well, done and done. I'd confessed, I'd believed, and I was saved. I wasn't going to hell. Pastor B said all I had to do now was try to be good. Even if I couldn't quite manage it, he seemed to think it was the thought that counted.

If it wasn't for the guilt, I might have been able to believe it. That cursed guilt that robbed me of more and more sleep as each new week rolled by. It was as though heaven itself was screaming that it demanded more, but more what? More effort? More repentance? I couldn't fathom how I could give more of either.

Maybe I just needed to make a choice. I opened my sock drawer and reached for what appeared to be a long abandoned pair of dress socks. I unfurled them and two microSD cards fell into my hand.

It seemed wrong that something so small and innocuous should wield such power over me. But as I held them in my hand, I could feel the pull. A silent, unimpeachable command that I yield to their siren call.

I wanted to be free of them, so I made the choice. Grabbing a pair of scissors from my desk, I quickly clipped both cards in half. It wasn't until I was staring at four pieces of silicon where there had previously been two that I realized my heart was pounding. I had waged a brief but epic battle and finally emerged victorious.

I dropped the fragments in the trash can and collapsed back on my bed. All of the SD cards were gone, and I told myself that would be the end of it. The next time Sim offered me one, I would just tell him, "No, thanks." I wouldn't judge, but I just couldn't do it any more.

It would be that easy.

That Sunday marked the first time that semester that I hadn't felt like a total hypocrite during church. It had been several days since my last SD card session, and the cursed things were finally gone.

Amy and her mom were still coming to church with us. Which was great, don't get me wrong. But it was getting annoying trying to hide my true feelings from Dad. Not being able to hold Amy's hand as she sat right next to me made it seem like the forty-minute sermon was twice as long.

I was thrilled come Monday morning's free period to be

sharing one of the library couches with Amy, her hand properly entwined with mine.

With her free hand, she pulled a dog-eared copy of *My Utmost for His Highest* from her backpack. It was disheartening to see how much progress she was making. Relatively speaking, I was way behind.

"Looks like you're making some good headway," I said, nodding to the book.

"Oh, I wish," she said. "It's my dad's old copy. I guess there were a lot of entries that really spoke to him. With midterms and the List and everything, I just haven't found much time to get to it yet."

I felt a little better knowing I wasn't the only one procrastinating.

"Yeah, me either," I admitted. "I tried to start reading a biography on John Wesley over the weekend. Didn't get very far."

"Boring?"

I groaned. "Yeah. I think it was written about five hundred years ago. The language is pretty thick."

Amy squeezed my hand. "You'll get through it. Maybe we should set a day each week to start working on our projects? We could meet at my house after school."

I nodded. Pushing through them together seemed like the least painful way to get the projects finished.

"You excited about tomorrow?" Amy asked.

"Tomorrow?"

"Yeah, with the Cult," she said.

At the end of the previous week's meeting, Mark had suggested the name. "It's perfect," he'd said. "Think about it. If our parents found out what we're starting to think about these things, they'd probably think we were in a cult. And *cult* itself is defined as 'a relatively small group of people having religious beliefs or practices regarded by others as strange or sinister.' It's perfect!"

Leave it to the dork to find humor in definitions. But Amy and Dani both agreed the definition was a perfect fit for our situation. So it stuck.

We'd also realized we were at the end of our questions, so it was decided we should all take the week to think about new questions.

Amy continued, "I'm dying to find out what they want to tackle next."

"Oh, yeah. Should be interesting." I tried to infuse the statement with more enthusiasm than I felt.

Amy wasn't buying it.

"Something wrong?" she asked.

"No, not wrong, exactly."

She smiled. "Oh, I'm convinced then. Everything's fine."

I never thought I'd meet anyone that could challenge Sim in the sarcasm department, but Amy had proven herself equally adept. Maybe more so.

I sighed. "I guess I just thought things would make more sense once I got some answers. That I'd feel closer to God somehow."

"You don't?" she asked.

I shook my head. "No. I'm having a hard time thinking of God as anything more than an abstraction. He's up there with his expectations, whatever they are, and I'm down here expected to perform. He might as well be Congress or the

President of the United States. He makes laws that I'm expected to follow, and I get punished if I don't. But I'm never going to really get to know him. I'm beginning to wonder if I'm even supposed to. I mean, people always talk about having a personal relationship with Jesus, but doesn't that seem odd? How do you have a relationship with someone who never talks back?"

Amy nodded. "Well, I guess that's your next question then."

"Ehh, I'm not sure I really want to ask that."

"What are you worried about? You think they won't like you because you have a question? I thought that was the whole point of this thing, to ask the questions we didn't feel free to ask anywhere else."

Her penchant for being right was starting to get a little annoying.

"I guess so," I said, trying to sound as non-committal as possible.

"Besides, you kinda promised to be honest. Remember, 'no question can remain unasked.' For all you know, Dani and Mark are wondering the same thing."

Not having any other intelligent response, I grunted.

"What about you?" I asked after a moment's pause. "Do you feel like you really know God? I mean beyond just reading about him. Do you think you know him as a person?"

She shrugged. "I think I used to. I felt like I did when my dad was still here. It was as though I kind of knew God through him. I don't know if that makes sense. I know I haven't felt close to God since he died. I guess I'm just hoping I'll find my way back there. I think the answers we've come to so far have helped. It at least seems possible now that God wasn't directly responsible for my dad dying. It'd make it easier to be close to him if I could stop thinking he was to blame."

I didn't answer. I couldn't. Now that I'd starting asking questions, I wondered if I'd ever be able to stop, and I didn't want to give voice to the one now bouncing around inside my head.

"Okay, you got all quiet again," Amy said. "What are you thinking?"

"It's nothing," I said, shaking my head.

She shook hers back at me. "Uh-uh. You've been open with me up till now. Don't stop."

I turned to look in her eyes. "I don't want to cause a problem for you."

"That's sweet, but if we're going to be any good to or for each other, we're going to have to trust each other to be able to deal with whatever questions we have. You can trust me. It's probably not something I haven't already asked for myself anyway."

I closed my eyes and took a breath. Opening them again, I said, "Just because God wasn't directly responsible for killing your dad, I mean…he's still all-powerful, right? He could have stopped it, but he didn't. Isn't letting an innocent person get killed when you have the power to stop it just as bad as pulling the trigger yourself?"

Amy offered a small, mirthless smile. "I've wondered the exact same thing. Looks like we both have our next questions."

❖   ❖   ❖

By Tuesday night, the weather had turned, and the cloudy weather reflected my mood.

This time Mark beat us to the jazz room, but Dani was missing. He told us she wouldn't be able to be there that week because her sister, Marie, was getting married on Saturday.

"Dani's the maid of honor," Mark explained. "And Marie's starting to lose her mind a little bit. We had a get-together over the weekend, and it looked like Marie was going to spontaneously combust."

It felt a little weird having a meeting with just the three of us. Not quite the intimacy of a one-on-one conversation, but not enough people to really qualify as a group discussion. Hoping to get some questions and wrap up quickly, I asked who wanted to start us off.

After a moment of silence, Amy said to Mark, "I guess the biggest thing you and Dani don't know about me yet is that my mom and I moved here because my dad died about eight months ago. We have family here, and Mom especially needed to be closer to them."

"I'm sorry," Mark said. "That's awful."

Amy smiled. I wondered how she always managed to do that. When I got sad, or mad, or depressed, or anything like that, it was like someone tied twenty-pound barbells to the corners of my mouth. But Amy always managed to find a smile.

"Thanks," she said. "We're past the initial wave of it, but it has raised some questions. Before the last couple of weeks,

I was really struggling with how God could decide to kill my dad. I'm hopeful now that he didn't, but the fact remains that if God is all-powerful then he could have stopped it from happening. He didn't. My dad was a good person, and he died saving other people's lives. Why did God let it happen? Why does he let any of the terrible things in this world happen when he has the power to stop them? He could prevent every rape, every murder…but he doesn't. I'd like to know why."

Mark nodded slowly. "That's a tough one. I have a cousin that stopped going to church after his brother was killed in a car accident. He asked the same question and was never satisfied with the answers he got. People would say things like, 'Well, God has a plan we just can't understand.' I've never seen him as mad as he got in those moments."

I opened a notebook and started to write. "'Question 3: how can a good God allow all of the pain and suffering we see in the world?' Does that pretty much sum it up?"

Amy and Mark nodded.

"All right, then. I guess I'll go next if that's okay."

"Sure thing," Mark said.

There was silence again until I cleared my throat. "Well," I said with a deep breath. "I told Amy a bit about this yesterday. I've always struggled a bit with the idea of having a relationship with God. He just doesn't seem all that relatable to begin with, and I've never been able to wrap my head around the idea of knowing someone based on a book. I mean, take George Washington. I can know about him, but barring some impressive scientific advancements, I'll never be able to know him. It feels that way with God, that unless he actually starts talking back, I'll never really *know* him. So, I guess my question is this: am I even supposed to? Does God intend for us to truly have a personal relationship with him, or are we just supposed to thank him for saving us from hell and do what he says until we die? Does that make any sense?"

"I think so," Mark said. "And it plays into a question I've been thinking about." He swallowed hard. "Dani already knows this, but I've been struggling with lust for a long time. Sometimes I do okay with it for a while, and sometimes I don't. I talked to my youth pastor about it, and he said that pretty much all guys wrestle with it these days. I always feel guilty about it. He suggested I try to find an accountability partner, and try harder to stop. Nothing's really helped much. So, my question is about what salvation is even for. Are Christians supposed to be able to stop sinning? Can we be better, or just forgiven?"

I was stunned. I couldn't believe that Mark had just admitted that. I felt like I would die of shame if anyone, especially Amy, knew about the SD cards.

"Then I think we can probably combine these two questions." I started writing again. "'Question 4: what should life look like for a believer, specifically in regard to a relationship with God and the battle with sin?' Sound good?"

They both nodded again.

"Okay, then. Unless anyone else has a burning question that they need to get out now, I think these should provide us with plenty of study fodder for the next week. Any objections?"

Silence.

"Then, there we go. Questions 3 and 4. I'll make copies and email them out later. Sound good?"

"My parents monitor my email," Mark said.

Of course. My parents kept an eye on my browser history, but as far as I knew they didn't read my emails. Guess it wouldn't have surprised me if they did.

"It'd probably be safest just to keep everything on hard copy," Mark said. "Easier to hide it all.

I nodded, and Amy did, too. While neither Mark nor Dani had ever discussed their parents in detail, everyone was obviously nervous about what would happen if anyone discovered what we were doing out here.

I tucked the notebook safely in my backpack. Mark didn't need to worry. I was in no hurry for Dad to find out about this.

12

I had updated copies of *The List* for Mark and Dani when I ran into them on Wednesday. With four questions instead of the previous two, *The List* had begun to look as though it deserved its title.

Amy and I met at her house after school on Thursday to begin working on our term projects for Church History. I'd hoped that with two hours devoted solely to Wesley's biography, I might finally make some progress. And I did. Some. The presence of Amy Davidson proved to be the plan's fatal flaw. *The Life of John Wesley* was still hopelessly dull, and the game of footsie I was playing with Amy was far more enticing. I'd always rolled my eyes when I'd seen a couple at school do that and giggle at each other. Dumb as it had seemed then, I was beginning to understand its appeal.

I left her house that night only thirty pages further into Wesley's biography, but I was more in love with Amy than ever. I couldn't tell whether it was because we seemed to have so much in common, or whether it was due to our shared journey in questions of faith. Either way, I'd fallen for her more quickly than I would have believed possible.

Unfortunately, I hadn't done as good a job of hiding it from Dad as I'd thought. When I got home that night, I found him reading in the living room. And I got the distinct impression he'd placed himself there just to catch me the moment I came in the door.

"Hi,"

"Hey, Dad. Whatcha reading?" It was a weak misdirect.

"The new Grisham. Just starting it. Where you coming from?"

He made it sound like an innocuous question, but I knew better. I also knew better than to lie. It'd be too easy for him to verify where I'd been. "Amy's house. We were working on a class project for church history."

"Oh, yeah? You guys have a group project?"

Sometimes I could swear the man had learned his interrogation techniques from the CIA. He could make the process torturous and infuriating beyond belief.

"Not exactly. We both have a paper to research, and it seemed like it'd be more fun to work on it together than alone."

"Hm."

Not another word. Just *hm*. I wished he would just lay out his problem, but that had never been his method. I could elect to just say "good night" now and head to my room, but I knew that would only make things worse.

"We were just working on homework," I said, doing everything possible to keep the frustration out of my voice. "There's nothing wrong with that is there?"

From the look on Dad's face you'd think I'd just held up a convenience store or something.

"Nathan, we talked about this. I thought I'd made my feelings clear, but you seem intent on ignoring them."

"What do you mean?"

"You know perfectly well what I mean. Can you stand there and tell me in all honesty that you don't have feelings for this girl?"

Heck with it. It wasn't his business anyway. "Good grief, Dad. No, I don't have feelings for her."

"You expect me to believe that?" His tone was getting darker with each word.

"It's the truth."

Dad didn't respond. He just stared at me. I wouldn't have been surprised if he'd started growling.

"Good night," he said, finally, and turned his attention back to the novel without waiting for my response.

"Good night." I didn't bother trying to infuse the statement with any kind of sentiment. He wouldn't have believed it if I had.

I went straight to my room and closed the door. It was all I could do to keep from slamming it. I was five months away from adulthood, and he still thought he could run my life like I was nine years old. I usually felt bad lying to him, but this time I felt justified. He had no right acting that way, and I would definitely not give him the satisfaction of lording over me with another lecture about how irresponsible I was being. It's my FREAKING life! I can be as responsible or irresponsible as I want.

I imagine I must have looked a bit moronic as all of this

went through my mind. Sometimes you have to activate the pressure valve and blow some steam. Problem with your dad sitting right outside your bedroom door is that you have to do it quietly. So there I was, ranting in silence and gesturing like a lunatic at the ceiling and the dresser and the door and the desk. These things at least understood me.

Dad worked late Friday night. I wondered if he was as interested in avoiding me as I was in avoiding him. Maybe we could just orchestrate our schedules to not run into each other for the next seven months. I'd graduate high school, and we'd both be free of our respective burdens.

I felt a momentary pang of guilt at that thought. I imagined Amy saying something like, "At least you have a dad." Not that she ever would, but I suppose she'd be justified if she did. At the moment, I wasn't certain having a dad was worth the trouble.

Figuring it was my turn to play the avoidance card, I decided to give Sim a call Saturday morning after worship practice. A day spent frantically avoiding the undead seemed far more enjoyable than a day spent frantically avoiding Dad. Besides, it'd been a couple weeks since Sim had announced his agnosticism, and we hadn't really hung out since then.

I called from the phone in Pastor B's office, but it rang through to voice mail. So I called again, and this time it went to voicemail after just two rings.

Sim was surgically attached to his cell phone, so two calls

to voice mail was a little strange. I called his home line.

"Hello, Langford residence," answered a woman's voice.

"Hi Mrs. Langford, it's Rudy. Is Simon home?"

"Hi Rudy. Yes, he's in his room. Hold on a minute, and I'll get him."

A minute or two passed before I heard someone picking up the phone.

"Couldn't take the hint, huh?"

"What?"

Sim scoffed. "I know you're technologically challenged, but I would have thought that even you'd know when a call goes to voicemail after two rings, it means the person doesn't want to talk to you."

"So, you were…"

"Ignoring your calls," Sim interrupted. "Duh. You've been ignoring me for weeks, so I figured I'd let you see how it felt."

I knew we hadn't talked much lately, but I hadn't imagined he'd take it like this. "Sorry, man. Things have been a little crazy lately."

"Uh-huh. You seem to have plenty of time for Amy Davidson."

"What's that supposed to mean?"

"Exactly what it sounds like. At school, after school, the weekends… however crazy things are you seem to have plenty of time for new girlfriends. Guess old best friends take a back seat."

I knew he couldn't see me, but I rolled my eyes anyway. "Good grief, man. I'm sorry, okay. Things have just been a little nuts, and I guess I didn't realize. I was calling now to see if you wanted to hang out this afternoon."

"Haha, yeah, sure you were. Whatever, man. I've already got plans today. I'll see you at school."

The line went dead before I could say another word.

I strangled the handset and slammed it back down in the cradle. Between Dad and Sim, I was getting pretty fed up with people insisting I live my life on their terms.

Whatever. I didn't care if Sim really had plans or not. As long as he stayed in his current mood, I'd be happy to be somewhere else.

Which left Amy. Darn.

Unlike Sim, Amy picked up on the second ring.

I got to her house to find that Mrs. Davidson was out running errands and wouldn't be back for a few hours. Under normal circumstances, this would have given me pause. I've always been taught that it's both inappropriate and dangerous for a teenage guy and a teenage girl to be alone together. And, under normal circumstances, I might have agreed. But these weren't normal circumstances. I was more than a little fed up with people telling me how to live my life. I wanted to spend one freaking afternoon with my girlfriend without the world judging me, and trivial matters like her mom not being home were not going to stop me.

Amy opened the door within seconds of my knocking, but her smile evaporated upon seeing my face.

"What's wrong?"

I cracked a wry grin. "That obvious, huh?"

She nodded.

I collapsed on the living room sofa and gave an exasperated sigh. "I guess just about everything. Dad's on my case about spending time with you. He thinks I must be hellbent on wrecking my life because I decided to start hanging out with a girl."

"He doesn't approve?" she asked, sliding down onto the couch next to me.

I shook my head. "Not even remotely. He asked me point blank last night if I had feelings for you."

"What'd you tell him?"

"I lied to his face. How is it his business whether I have feelings for you or not?"

"You didn't tell him the truth?"

"No, I didn't! I didn't feel like standing there for another lecture about how I'm making terrible life choices and how God's not going to be honored by what I'm doing, or whatever. I'm sick of it!"

I could tell by the look on her face that I'd come off too harsh. I was angry, but not with her. That I was now taking my anger out on Amy just made me more livid at Dad.

"I'm sorry," I said, taking her hand. "I'm just a little fried. I tried calling Sim before coming over, and that didn't go very well either."

I filled her in on the details of my conversation with Sim. By the end of it, I was on edge again.

Amy got up from the couch. "Wait here a minute."

She headed into kitchen where I heard her rumbling around in one of the cupboards. She returned a moment later with two glasses.

And a bottle of vodka.

"Whoa, what are you doing?" I asked. Being home alone with Amy was one thing. Drinking was a whole other ball game.

"Relax," she said, as though this was the most natural thing in the world. "I'm not going to get you hammered."

She unscrewed the cap and poured a splash into each cup. Placing the bottle back on the table, she picked up the glasses and held one out to me. I didn't reach for it.

"Come on," she urged. "It's not going to bite you." She giggled. "Well, that's not entirely true. This stuff does have a bit of a kick to it."

"Why are you doing this?" I asked, still not reaching for the glass.

"Because you're seriously stressed out, and I know of no faster cure for stress than a shot or two of the good stuff."

I looked at her. She shrugged and held out the cup again. I took it, hesitant, and sniffed. "Isn't this wrong?" I asked. My folks had a glass of wine on occasion, but I'd never been allowed. Drinking under age was a strict no-no in our house.

"Not as far as I can tell," Amy said, still the paragon of nonchalance. "I mean, sure, maybe it's against the law. But biblically I can't find a problem with it. No where is drinking expressly forbidden. Drunkenness, sure, but not drinking."

"And you've done it before?" I was still having trouble processing this new development.

She nodded. "Ever since my dad died, I feel almost constantly tense. It's better when I'm with you, but it's still there. Sometimes it all gets a bit overwhelming. Mom had me talk to a Christian counselor, and they prescribed some antidepressants. I couldn't stand the way I felt on those. Besides, I wasn't depressed. Just tense. It's hard to explain. Anyway, growing up I'd seen Mom and Dad have a glass of vodka or wine or whatever after a rough day. I figured there had to be a reason. So one night after Mom had gone to bed I snuck into the kitchen and tried it."

"And it worked?"

She shrugged. "It's not perfect. But it's a bit like when I'm with you. It takes the edge off."

I looked at the liquid in my glass. If I hadn't just seen her pour it, I'd have sworn I was holding a cup of water.

On one hand, I felt certain this was a mistake. That I should head into the kitchen and dump the stuff in the sink. On the other hand, she was right about the stress, and it kept hitting harder. After every SD card session. After every encounter with Dad. Sometimes for seemingly no reason at all.

"I don't know," I said, running out of excuses.

"I did look it up," she said. "Paul actually told Timothy in one of his letters to take a little wine for his stomach. I figure if Timothy could have wine for his gut, I can have a little vodka for my nerves. Just avoid getting drunk, and we're not technically doing anything wrong."

Her logic, as per usual, was unassailable. "Okay…" I said. I lifted the glass and tipped it back, allowing the smallest amount of the drink to pass my lips. I swallowed, and proceeded to cough like a chronic smoker.

Amy found it hilarious.

"You did that on purpose, didn't you?" I said, fighting

for breath.

Amy was still fighting for hers, too. "Oh yes. I mean, I honestly think it'll help, but I figured you'd start hacking like that. I did the first time, too. Thought for certain Mom was going to wake up."

I regarded the cup. "That stuff is...wow."

"Right? Normally, I toss back about twice this amount, and I start feeling a bit better. Still completely in control, just a little more relaxed. You've never had it, so what's in your glass should be just about right."

I took another sip, this time better prepared for the effect. It burned as it slid down my throat. It had almost no flavor whatsoever, but the effect was more pleasant than I'd expected.

"Not bad," I admitted, tossing back the rest.

Amy drained her glass and took everything back to the kitchen. The bottle was about half full, and I watched as she cleaned the glasses and put everything back where it had been.

"I try to ration my doses based on when Mom drinks it. But this bottle's right at the halfway mark, so she won't notice a couple of shots missing."

We headed back to the living room, and Amy flipped on the TV. I put my arm around her, and she surfed the channels before finally landing on a *Gilligan's Island* rerun. About two minutes in I started feeling warm. It was weird, though. I felt warm *inside*. I couldn't think of anything in my experience to compare it to. Everything felt a little lighter.

"I think it's working," I said.

"See? It's like taking aspirin for a headache. Your body's

a bit off, and this fixes it."

I did feel better, not to mention way more relaxed than I'd been in weeks.

We sat there, her head against my shoulder, until the episode ended. I didn't ever want to move, but I couldn't help thinking about what would happen if her mom came back.

"Should we go somewhere?" I asked. "I mean, won't your mom be upset if she comes home and finds me here?"

Amy shook her head. "Not a chance. I mean, yeah, she'd probably blow a gasket, but she won't be home until later. She's having dinner out with her sister, so we've got time."

Another episode started, and I settled back into the couch, perfectly content to stay right where I was.

After the third episode of what had turned out to be a *Gilligan's Island* marathon, Amy muted the TV.

"Why do you like me?"

I turned to face her and raised an eyebrow. "Really?"

She nodded. "Really."

"Sorry," I said. "Just seemed a little outta left field. I don't know, I guess I like you for a lot of reasons."

"Such as?"

I laughed, feeling a little awkward about this sudden turn in the conversation. "Well, I guess it's partly because you seem to get me. You understand why I ask the questions I do. I can just talk to you without having to worry about how you're going to judge me for something I don't understand. I feel safe with you. I can be me without having to pretend that I'm anyone else. Beyond that, I think you're amazing. You know your way around the clarinet, you steal swigs from your mom's vodka bottle, you could probably host your own Twitch channel with those Call of Duty skills, and you're one of the smartest people I know."

Amy was blushing and glanced away. "Is that all?"

"Well," I said, taking the blushing as a good sign. "You're also the most beautiful girl walking around Lakewood. That might have a little something to do with it."

She blushed again. "Mr. Rudolph, you're a tease."

I smiled. "Learned it from you. But what about you? Why do you like me?"

She shrugged. "Well, you're really the only boy I know here at all, so…"

"Nice," I said, half-feigning offense.

"I'm kidding." She smiled at me. "I like you because you're an easy target. You're honest. You're cute. You're handsome and thoughtful. I like you for all those reasons, and because I can't think of a single reason not to."

I smiled, and she smiled back at me. So many of my relationships were falling apart, but this one thing worked. Amy was all I needed. All I wanted. Every movie and TV show gave the idea that my next words would be hard to say, that they somehow meant I'd be bound to something and unable to escape.

But that's exactly what I wanted.

"I love you, Amy," I said brushing a strand of her brown hair from her eyes.

I thought she'd blush again, but she didn't. She looked

right back into my eyes, just inches from hers, and said, "I love you, too."

Then the inches vanished, and I could feel her lips against mine. I had never kissed a girl in my life, and I don't know what I expected. Whether a result of our mutually professed love or the alcohol still working in my system, the world faded away as we kissed.

I don't know how long we stayed like that. She finally pulled back, just an inch.

"Wow…"

She smiled. "That's what you said about the vodka."

I laughed. "Yeah, but the vodka was just, wow. This was…*wow.*"

She looked a little shy. "We should probably stop, huh?"

Stopping was the last thing I wanted to do, but she was right. Mrs. Davidson still wasn't due home for hours, but if her plans changed and she walked in to find us making out on the couch…yeah, that wouldn't end well.

So, I nodded. "You hungry?" The clock on the wall read 2:04.

"Actually, yeah," she said, rising from the couch and stretching. "You wanna go somewhere?"

We settled on the Mile-Hi Diner. I was a bit hesitant to drive while still feeling the vodka's effects, so I gave Amy the keys. She had far more experience with alcohol than I did, and it seemed like Otis would be in better hands with her behind the wheel.

Thick cloud cover gave the afternoon a cold, heavy feeling. The evening's forecast called for six inches of snow. Just about every year, the Colorado winter puts on an early show, as though prepping us all for what's to come. Late October was a bit earlier than usual, but no one was all that surprised.

The wind started picking up as we walked in to the diner. We ordered a pair of bacon cheeseburger combos and settled into a corner booth. I tried kissing Amy again between bites.

"Oh, gross!"

"*Gross?*" I said, somewhat indignant. "Really?"

"I'm sorry," she said laughing. "You just taste like cheeseburger. It's kinda gross."

I couldn't help but laugh along with her. I resisted the urge to tell her that she tasted like cheeseburger, too, and I just didn't care. Instead, I focused on eating as fast as I could, and for no other reason than so I could kiss her again.

13

Finally feeling clear-headed, I drove Amy home after lunch. Her mom hadn't returned, and likely wouldn't until after dinner. Still, we decided it wasn't a good idea for me to stick around. We'd have some uncomfortable questions to answer if Mrs. Davidson got home and I was still there.

So, we stole inside for a few minutes and kissed again. I didn't want to leave. Ever. Amy maintained a firmer grip on reality, though, and after a few minutes she pushed me out the front door with a laugh, said goodbye, and locked it.

I turned to walk toward Otis and nearly had a heart attack when I saw Sim standing there.

He laughed.

I put a hand to my chest in a vain attempt to steady my heartbeat.

"Not cool, man. What the heck are you doing here?"

Sim was still laughing. "Oh, man. The wait was worth it just for that."

"Ha ha. Seriously, what are you doing here?"

Sim rolled his eyes. "Relax, dude. I knew you'd get around to making out with her eventually."

"Did you see us?" I asked, starting to panic. I spun back to the house to see if I could see inside the windows.

"Not a bit. You just confirmed it, though. Nice work."

I turned back to Sim, fuming and feeling more than a little invaded. I moved around to the driver's side and opened the door.

"Oh, for crying out loud, would you just chill out for a second?" Sim said. "I did come all the way over here to talk to you."

"About what?" I said, my patience spent.

"About earlier. I...I wanted to apologize." Sim's eyes fell. It wasn't a posture he adopted that often. His cocky attitude tended to prevent any kind of penitent display.

"Oh."

"Yeah," he said, still looking at the hood of the car. The cold and his embarrassment had lent his cheeks a reddish tint that almost matched his hair. "Look, I'm sorry about going off on you on the phone. I know you're a little smitten right now. I guess I was just feeling left out, and it got to me."

I leaned on Otis's roof with both arms and sighed. "I'm sorry, too. I wasn't trying to ignore you. I guess I got kinda swept up in the whole thing, you know?"

Sim chuckled. "Yeah, I know. It's kinda funny to watch, actually."

"So, I guess we've transitioned from apologies to insults?"

"Come on, like that was gonna take long." Sim smacked

the hood of the car. "So, you wanna bring your sorry, 'swept-up' carcass over to my place for some CoD or what?"

I nodded. "Sounds good."

Curse you, Sim.

As Saturdays go, this one had been just about perfect. Minus having to get up early for worship practice, I'd had an amazing time with Amy, and Sim and I were just about back to normal.

And to top it off, I outscored Sim ten out of sixteen rounds of zombies. Life was good.

Then the idiot had to go and open his mouth.

"So, dude," he said after I finished shellacking him in round seventeen. "Have you heard about this new web browser?"

Leave it to Sim to screw up an otherwise excellent evening of zombie slaying by going uber-nerd.

"New web browser?" I asked, incredulous. "Seriously?"

"Oh, yeah. It's called Xpedition. It's got everything you'd want from a browser. It's crazy fast, has tabbed browsing, auto-translate features, and solid-bookmarking. But the real kicker is Stealth Mode."

I raised an eyebrow, trying to convey that the conversation had migrated into the absurd. "Stealth Mode?"

"Uh-huh," he said, nodding with this stupid smirk like he'd just stumbled on the greatest thing ever. "Check this out."

Sim grabbed his laptop from the side table and opened a

new Xpedition window. "You just go to the menu and select Stealth Mode. The window's border darkens letting you know that you're totally untrackable."

"I don't get it. You that afraid of someone knowing where you are? Call me crazy, man, but I doubt the FBI cares much about the movements of a seventeen-year-old drop-out risk."

"Ah, Rudy, Rudy, Rudy…" Sim had adopted his you're-so-lucky-you-have-me-here tone. "We really have to bring you out of the technological dark ages. Stealth Mode encrypts your browsing activity. No matter where you go or what you do online, nothing is saved. No browsing history, no cookies, no record of any downloaded files. You're completely invisible."

Two hours later, I was sitting in my room cursing Sim's name, parentage, birth…pretty much everything about the guy. No sooner had I finally kicked the SD cards to the curb than my laptop itself had taken their place. My parents had always insisted on regular checks of my browsing history. They may not be technological geniuses, but they're not stupid. They know the world. And the knowledge that they were going to see where I'd been online had thus far been sufficient incentive to keep me away from anything like what Sim loaded onto the SD cards.

Just like that, with one miserable technological "advancement", all fear of ever getting caught was gone. And once again, it was just me against the temptation.

I sat on my bed staring at the computer screen for what seemed like hours. It was like we were engaged in a *Princess Bride*-style battle of wits.

To the death.

Finally, I opened a browser and started to download Xpedition. I told myself that I wanted to test out the auto-translate feature, and see if it really was as fast as Sim said.

It was fast, I guess, and it seemed like its version of tabbed browsing was smooth and convenient.

But of course, it was never really about either of those things.

And Stealth Mode worked just as advertised.

2:37a

The faint red numbers glimmered in the darkness, taunting me. "Hey Rudy, guess what? Just five more hours until you have to get up and head to church!"

I groaned and rolled over, but it was pointless. Sleep wasn't coming any time soon.

A mere week of being free of this thing, and now I was back in its unyielding grasp. I wondered if it had ever let me go, or if it was just toying with me. Like a cat letting a mouse get halfway back to its hole before pouncing in for the kill.

I rolled onto my face and screamed into the pillow. All the frustration I felt toward Dad, church, school, continuing to lose this fight, and now insomnia…it all boiled up in a steaming cauldron. The pressure was rising, and screaming into the night seemed the only logical action.

Mark's questions played in my head as if set on a permanent loop.

Are Christians supposed to be able to stop sinning? Can we be better, or are we just forgiven?

At the moment, I was definitely leaning toward just forgiven. Better seemed impossibly out of reach.

But, the whole point of this Cult thing was to find out if the Bible could give any clarity to these questions. I rolled over and looked at the clock again.

2:54a

Sleep was out of the question. I crawled off the foot of the bed and grabbed my Bible and laptop from the desk. Sitting back on the bed, I wasn't even sure where to begin. I popped on my reading lamp and opened the laptop. A blank search bar stared back at me.

Are Christians supposed to be able to stop sinning?

A bit on the nose, perhaps. But I was sleep deprived, and it seemed as good a place as any to start looking.

To my surprise, it kicked back page after page of people answering that exact question. I clicked on the top few links and read through the various answers. Without fail, they all came back to Romans 7. The pertinent passage seemed to be verses 14-19:

> *We know that the law is spiritual; but I am unspiritual, sold as a slave to sin. I do not understand what I do. For what I want to do I do not do, but what I hate I do. And if I do what I do not want to do, I agree that the law is good. As it is, it is no longer I myself who do it, but it is sin living in me. For I know that good itself does not dwell in me, that is, in my sinful nature. For I have the desire to do what is good, but I cannot carry it out. For I do not do the good I want to do, but the evil I do not want to do - this I keep on doing.*

It made sense, mainly because it summed up my entire

struggle with lust. I wanted to do the right thing, but it was always just out of reach. On the other hand, everything that I didn't want to do, those things wielded an unbreakable control over me.

And why shouldn't they? What was it Paul wrote? *For I know that good itself does not dwell in me, that is, in my sinful nature?* If my nature is sinful, how could I ever hope to defeat that? Not like you see a lot of vegetarian lions out there. Their nature is to pick off the weak gazelles, and that's what they do.

Each site seemed pretty much in line with the others. Because of our sin nature, we can't be good. So we have to rely on Christ having been good for us. Through faith, his righteousness is imputed to us, and we're counted as righteous, too.

It all sounded great, and pretty much in line with what Pastor B had said.

Except for this. It was now 3:42 a.m., and I still couldn't sleep. The guilt kept eating at me. And if it didn't matter whether or not I stopped sinning, then why all of the verses like Philippians 2:12b, "…work out your salvation with fear and trembling." Or I Corinthians 9:24, "Do you not know that in a race all the runners run, but only one gets the prize? Run in such a way as to get the prize." If I can't stop sinning, then what difference does it make how hard I try?

With the clock nearing 4:30 a.m., I found a site that focused its answer on I Corinthians 3:11-15:

For no one can lay any foundation other than the one already laid, which is Jesus Christ. If anyone builds on this foundation using gold, silver, costly stones, wood, hay or straw, their work will be shown for what it is, because the Day will bring it to light. It will be revealed with fire, and the fire will test the quality of each person's work. If what has been built survives, the builder will receive a reward. If it is burned up, the builder will suffer loss, but yet will be saved - even though only as one escaping through the flames.

The author of this site explained that while Christ handles the work of saving us, what we do after that is on us. It doesn't have any bearing on whether or not we're saved. It just impacts our eternal reward.

It felt like I was starting to get a full picture, and it fit with everything I'd been experiencing. I can't always overcome sin. Sometimes I might win, other times I won't. But sin is my nature, so it's always going to be a struggle, and I'm probably always going to be outmatched. But as long as I believe in Christ and trust him to take care of my sin, I'll ultimately be okay. If I failed too often in the fight against sin, then I just wouldn't have a very big reward. I'd still escape eternal torment.

I took a deep breath. If I was understanding this right, then it was a huge relief. So I might not have a huge mansion in heaven. I could live with that. As long as hell was out of the picture, I could deal with the rest.

I opened a new Word document and quickly typed up my thoughts, then printed them out using the ancient printer my dad let me keep when he'd upgraded the previous year. I tried reading over them to see if they made sense, but I was now finding it hard to stay awake.

I shoved the paper in my backpack, set my Bible and computer on the floor, and switched off the lamp. The clock now read *5:15a*, but I felt like I might finally be able to sleep.

14

My alarm went off at 7:30 a.m.

And again at 7:38 a.m.

7:46 a.m.

7:54 a.m.

It's hard to say whether the snooze button is the greatest or worst invention in human history. Either way, by 8:02 a.m. I had delayed getting up for as long as I could.

I threw my clothes on in a haze, foregoing the tie. Dad was always big on "giving God our very best." Today God was getting me on two hours of sleep. My best was not in the cards.

Dad was at the table with his Bible and a bowl of bran flakes. I mumbled a "Good morning," grabbed a package of Pop Tarts from the cupboard, and headed out the door.

The whole morning passed in a fog. When I arrived at church, I suddenly realized I couldn't remember a single moment of the drive there. Breathing a quick prayer of thanks that I'd arrived in one piece, I headed into the sanctuary and worked my way through practice. I made more mistakes than usual, and Gary shot me a look at one point. I made it a point to drink two full cups of coffee during Sunday school. I felt a tad more awake during the actual service and managed a better performance.

By the time church ended, I was ready to pass out. I warred against my eyelids throughout the entire sermon, and when it was over I couldn't remember what it'd been about. I told my folks I'd see them at home, and left.

The drive home presented its own battle as I fought to keep my eyes on the road and Otis in his lane. I wondered if that was what it felt like to drive drunk, sort of in control, but sort of not. I made a mental note to never find out.

When Otis pulled into the drive, we were both still intact. The house was quiet, and I was asleep within minutes of hitting the mattress.

I slept straight through Sunday afternoon and evening. At one point I dreamed that someone else was in my room, but the image never resolved into an actual person.

Of course, the problem with sleeping all that time is that your body decides it's done sleeping long before morning arrives. So when I woke up Monday morning and rolled over to look at the clock...

4:32a

Ugh...

I laid there for a while trying to will myself back to sleep, but by 5:05, it was pretty clear I was awake for the day.

With hours to kill, I decided it was as good a time as any to force my way through more of Wesley's biography. It was still boring to the point of mind-numbing, but I had six weeks left to finish the project. I needed to learn *something* about the guy that would make for a decent reflection paper.

From the bit I had learned about him so far, it didn't seem that Wesley and I could have been more different if we'd tried. Faith seemed impossible for me. It just seemed to work for him. He did what he was supposed to. He went to church, went to school to study the Bible, was ordained as a preacher and even led a group called the Holy Club. Every day they spent at least 3 hours in prayer and Bible study.

I can't help but wonder what that would be like. How could you keep up that level of commitment without burning yourself out? It seemed like there had to be something more to Wesley's faith, some key ingredient that he'd discovered that I never had.

I started to worry about the project. If I had to start it now, it'd be a short paper. Write about something in his life that really affected me on a personal level? Thus far, all I had was, "He seemed really committed. I wish I could feel that way."

Not, I think, the inspiring treatise Ms. Waller was hoping for.

I slipped out of the house at six and headed to school for some pre-class piano time.

By mid-afternoon, I was ready to pass out again. Kissing

Amy whenever we were sure no one was watching in free period had been the day's high water mark, and now all I wanted was more sleep.

At the final bell, I told Amy goodbye and headed straight home, intent on grabbing a couple hours of sleep before dinner. As I came through the front door, however, I was immediately struck by the image of both Mom and Dad sitting in the living room. It was clear from their postures that they'd been waiting for me, and there was a heaviness to the air.

"Did someone die?" I asked.

"Come sit down, Rudy," Mom said, in a tone that neither confirmed nor denied my question.

"What's going on?" I asked, moving to the couch across from them. "Seriously, you guys are freaking me out."

Dad looked at me, and I could see now that his expression was not one of grief, but anger.

"You mother and I would like to know what you've been doing after school on Tuesdays."

My heart started pounding in my chest. There was no way he could know what we'd been doing in the jazz room.

"Amy and I have been hanging out. You know, homework stuff." A little truth, a little lie. It was a kind of homework, after all.

"Where have you been doing this hanging out and homework stuff?" Dad asked, his tone seeming a little darker than before.

I wasn't sure how to answer. If I told him we'd been hanging out at Amy's house, a single call to Mrs. Davidson would confirm that I was lying. If I told him the truth...well, that wasn't an option.

"Starbucks, mostly."

"Hmm," Dad nodded. How he managed imbue even a simple nod with sarcasm amazed me. "Well, if you've been spending Tuesdays at Starbucks hanging out and working on homework stuff, I suppose you wouldn't be able to tell me anything about these?"

Dad slapped two pieces of paper down on the coffee table. A quick glance confirmed my fears.

Moron, I silently berated myself. Like an idiot, I'd titled my thoughts on question 3, "Notes for Tuesday's Cult Meeting." I'd thought I was being clever.

Then I remembered my dream. "It was you in my room on Sunday. You went through my backpack?"

"Yes, I did," Dad replied, clearly not feeling like he'd done anything wrong. "And I'd like to know exactly what this cult is."

My blood ran hot, his violation fueling my anger. "It's none of your business."

Dad's eyes widened. "Excuse me? You live in my house, young man. That makes this very much my business, and you *will* answer me."

He stared me down, and I stared right back. I felt outgunned, and I was going to be grounded forever. But I'd stay grounded until graduation before I gave up the rest of the Cult.

"When did this rebellion start, Nathan?" Dad asked. I guess the question was rhetorical because he immediately asked, "If you won't tell me about this cult, then maybe you can explain this?" He picked up the List and snapped it taut in front of me.

I looked back at him. Part of me felt intimidated, scared of what he would do if I continued to challenge him. In the past, I'd always backed down, always yielded to his stronger will.

But that was then. And I decided no matter the consequences, I wasn't backing down this time.

"What do you want to know?" I asked, forcing as much nonchalance into my voice as I could. "Seems pretty self-explanatory to me."

"Do not be flippant with me!" he demanded, his voice rising in both volume and frustration. "I want to know who you've been talking to about these questions. Why didn't you bring them to me?"

"Gee, Dad, I wonder. Maybe I prefer talking with people that won't start yelling at me the moment they disagree with something I've said."

I could tell I'd pushed a button. Dad didn't say anything right away, and it looked like he was channeling all of his energy toward not losing it. So Mom stepped in.

"Nathan, please show your father the respect he deserves. You've been going behind our backs. At the very least, you owe us an explanation."

Part of me knew that she had a point, but that part had already lost out to the raging, righteously indignant part.

"No. This is my business and mine alone. Rather than just talk to me, you know, actually take the time to know me, you went through my things digging around for God knows what, *while I was asleep*! And you're *surprised* that I wasn't completely open and honest with you? Look, ground me if you want, but I'm not saying anything more about the Cult or The List." I fell silent, returning my Dad's fiery gaze, determined that I wouldn't be the first to look away.

I won. Dad's eyes fell, and he looked toward Mom. Finally, he stood up and held out a hand, saying, "Give me your backpack."

"What? So you can go through my stuff again?"

"Nathan! *Give me the backpack!*" He reached out and grabbed it from me. I released my grip without a fight, somewhat stunned by his physical display. For the first time in my life, I wondered if he was capable of hitting me.

Dad rifled through the pockets for a minute, then said, "Your cell phone. I want that, too."

As committed as I was to holding my ground, I wasn't sure I wanted this to come to blows. I held it out, but far enough away that he had to take an extra step forward to retrieve it.

"You *are* grounded."

"Imagine my surprise," I said, invoking every bit of the sarcasm I'd learned from him over the years.

Dad glared at me. Actually, I'm not sure he'd stopped glaring at me since the beginning of this little encounter. "Oh, keep it up, smart guy. You'll remain in your room except to go to the bathroom until you've rethought your entire course here. And until I feel like you've reached a point of genuine repentance, you will stay there. You will go to church with us on Sunday, but you will not play with the worship team. You will not go to school. I'll be speaking with your teachers and will pick up your homework, but I guarantee if you don't get back to school soon your chances of graduating this spring will be severely jeopardized."

My mouth had fallen open an inch. I had expected a grounding, but this was going way further than I'd imagined. For a moment I considered railing against the unfairness of it, but I forced my mouth shut. Hell would freeze over before I gave him the satisfaction.

Without another word, I stood up from the couch, went to my room, and slammed the door.

Mom brought me a plate of dinner, and I passed a long afternoon and evening alone. On the occasions that I had to venture forth to use the bathroom, I made it a point to keep my eyes down. My father was the last thing in the world I wanted to see.

As the night wore on, I began to wonder if he'd actually hold his position. A grounding made sense. But actually keeping me out of school? Would he really jeopardize my future over this? By the time I fell into a fitful sleep, I was convinced that come morning he'd relent and let me go to school.

But he surprised me. I woke up early, just in case. I showered and dressed, and was sitting on the edge of my bed flipping absent-mindedly through Wesley's biography when Mom came in with a bowl of cereal.

"So, he's actually serious about this?" I asked, indignant.

"No, Nathan. *We* are serious about this. Your attitude is out of control, and we're deeply worried about you. This has to stop."

Turning my attention to the bowl of cereal, I started eating as though she wasn't standing there. After a moment, she turned and left the room. I felt bad about giving Mom the cold shoulder, but I wasn't going to be the one to back down.

Of course, I'd been grounded before, but this felt different. I imagined what Sim and Amy were doing at school and wondered whether they were talking together in the hallway wondering where I was. They'd probably both tried to text and call. What did they think when I didn't respond?

So passed one of the longest days of my life as I alternated between reading and pacing and lying on the bed or the floor and staring at the ceiling. How long could Dad really keep this up? March 16th would mark my eighteenth birthday. It was five months away. Would he keep me locked up until then? Would he try for longer? I decided if it came down to it, I'd leave home the day I turned eighteen. By then I'd probably need remedial work to finish high school, but what the heck? Maybe I could just take the GED and be done with it. Sim would let me crash with him until I could afford a place of my own. College might have to wait a while, but if I started working full time I could probably get a studio apartment of my own and take it from there.

Any scenario now seemed better than spending one more day at home than I had to.

Dad's car rolled into the driveway around 3:45 p.m. It was somewhat surprising given that his work days normally ended around 4:30. He didn't keep me in suspense for long. Without the courtesy of a knock, he came barging into my room almost as soon as he entered the house.

"Nathan."

"Dad."

He nodded. "Still holding on to that rebellious streak, huh? Well, seeing as you were unwilling to offer any answers, I decided to get them for myself. When I went to Knight's Day to pick up your homework, I asked if anyone had seen you go anywhere after classes on Tuesdays. Took a little while, but I found out about the jazz room. I have to say, Nathan, I am amazed at the level of arrogance displayed by you and your friends in there. To reject what you've been taught by your parents and pastors in favor of the counsel of a bunch of other teenagers?"

I had trouble keeping up, still a little hung on the fact that he'd actually gone to my school. Was there no limit to how far this man would go to invade my privacy?

"Your friends were a bit surprised when I opened the door. Amy was there, though I'm certain now that comes as no surprise to you, and there was another young man and woman I recognized from events at your school. Your mother and I will be discussing all of this with Mrs. Davidson tonight, and I'll be going through your yearbook to find the names of the other kids. I think their parents deserve to know what their children have been up to."

I sat stone silent on the bed. Even if I'd wanted to respond, I was too stunned. It didn't matter that I'd tried to fall on the sword for the rest of the Cult. Dad was going to wreck everything we'd done, all because he was bent out of shape that I wouldn't tell him what he wanted to know. As if someone with his cheating record had the right to assume such a high-and-mighty, holier-than-thou position.

After a minute, Dad seemed to decide that he'd said his piece. He left the room, closing the door firmly behind him.

I knew then that whatever relationship I'd still had with my Dad was over. He was now Adam Rudolph, and beyond a last name and a house for the next five months, we would never share anything again.

15

I was living out my own personal version of *Groundhog Day*. Tuesday rolled slowly into Wednesday which eventually became Thursday. By that point I'd started envying Bill Murray's character. At least he got to cut loose.

Midway through Friday morning, I started wondering again how long Adam would keep this up.

Oh, yeah. Adam. "Dad" was too personal. Adam was easier to hate. And I was in a hating mood.

I hated him for invading my privacy. I hated him for caring so little about the things that mattered to me that I'd been forced to be private about all of it in the first place. I hated him for treating me like a child, when for all intents and purposes I was a functional adult now...

Wait. *I'm a functional adult now.* What could Adam actually do if I just left my room and did whatever I pleased? Nothing. He could yell at me. Try to intimidate me back into my room. But he couldn't *make* me go. He could keep the computer and cell phone. Even the car. He'd given me those and could take them away. But he couldn't actually force me to do anything. Unless he resorted to violence, in which case I could call the cops.

I wondered if I could take it that far. Probably wouldn't have to. Just threaten it, and Adam would cave. If he didn't, then I'd have no qualms about calling five-oh.

The decision was easy from there. I was going stir-crazy staring at the same four walls, and it was already going to take a ton of work to catch up on my classes. Zach had brought my homework in each afternoon, but it wasn't the same as being there.

Mom was out running errands, Dad was at work, and Zach was at school. Escaping the confines of my suburban prison required only the will to walk out a door.

I gathered my school books, brushed my hair for the first time in days, and left.

During the three-mile walk to school, I felt liberated. Beyond free. It wasn't just that I was finally outside the confines of my bedroom. Every line my father had ever drawn, the hard rules, the disapproving glances, the judgmental tones...for the first time in my life I was beyond all of it. It couldn't touch me. I might as well have been Andy Dufresne driving with the top down to Zihuatanejo.

I got to school right at 10:00, just in time to catch Amy walking into the library.

"Rudy!" she cried, running up to me. She threw her arms around me, and I spun her around.

"I missed you," I said, kissing her forehead.

She looked up at me. "Zach told me you were grounded, but he couldn't say much more than that. What happened?"

I sighed, and pulled her into the library. We found our customary couch toward the back of the room and settled in.

"My father lost all touch with reality," I began. "I guess he thought we were hooking up or something, so he went through my backpack looking for evidence. He found *The List* and some notes I'd typed up for Tuesday. Like an idiot, I'd left enough information on the page that he was able to piece it together. When I got home from school on Monday, he and Mom were waiting for me. He started asking me all these questions as though he didn't already know exactly where I'd been. I said you and I had been hanging out and doing homework stuff. He didn't buy that, obviously, and threw out the stuff from the Cult. I wouldn't answer any of his questions after that, so he took my computer and cell phone and grounded me. I've been sitting in my bedroom for the last three days."

"Wow," Amy whispered, her face sympathetic. "He finally let you out?"

I shook my head. "Nope. Just decided I wasn't going to sit there any more."

"Isn't he going to be angry?"

"Oh, I expect he'll be furious. It just doesn't matter anymore. He told me what he did on Tuesday, but what happened after that?"

"Well, I guess you already know that he came to the jazz room. He gave us all a big speech about how arrogant we were being and how he was going to make certain that all of our parents knew what we were doing. He told us all to leave, but nobody moved at first. He said he wasn't leaving until we were all gone. Mark tried to engage him on some of the questions, but your dad wasn't interested. He just insisted again that we were all leaving. We didn't really have much choice."

I realized my fists were clenched and forced them to relax. "I still can't believe he actually did that."

"It was pretty weird," Amy agreed. "I guess he called my mom that night because she came into my room and confronted me about it. I'd known it was coming, but it was still hard figuring out what to say. She took it better than I expected. Said she was hurt that I hadn't trusted her with what I was thinking and feeling, but that she was sorry I'd felt like I couldn't talk to her about my questions."

My mouth fell open. "Wait, your mom actually *apologized* to you?"

Amy nodded.

"Wow. You really do have the coolest mom ever."

Amy gave a gentle grin. "Yeah. Unfortunately, the other parents didn't take it so well. Mark's grounded, and Dani's parents are thinking about taking her out of school."

"And it's all my fault."

She squeezed my hand. "Come on, there's no way you could have known your dad would do that."

I shook my head. "I should have seen it coming. I knew he was getting suspicious about us. He suspected that I had feelings for you. I just didn't think he was capable of taking it that far. Everything we've worked for, gone because my old man has a disturbing need to control me."

"Well, I wouldn't say that."

I raised an eyebrow. "What do you mean?"

"Mark figured it out. Instead of weekly meetings, he set up a private forum online. He created logins for everyone in the Cult. He gave me yours. You're supposed to memorize it, then throw the card away. Here."

She handed me a small, square piece of paper. It gave a web address and login information:

Username: RudRud
Password: D0ntSwe4t1t

"Huh," I said.

"What?"

"The password."

Amy smiled. "Oh, yeah. We did manage to talk a little on Wednesday. They both felt bad for you. Nobody blames you for what happened."

"I guess I couldn't fault them if they did."

"Stop it." I could feel Amy looking at me, waiting for me to turn and meet her gaze. When I finally did, she said, "It's done. You can't undo it. We have a way to continue, and that's all that matters right now."

I looked at her, thanking God that she was here. With me.

"I love you."

"I know," she said, her grin taking on a flirtatious air that made me want to kiss her.

So, I did. The couch was hidden from the librarian's

desk, and I hadn't heard anyone else come into the library since we'd sat down. I lost myself in her lips. Amy finally pulled back after a few minutes and looked around to make sure no one was watching. I followed her searching gaze around the room, then moved to kiss her again. She put a hand up to my lips.

"Not here. We're in enough trouble already, don't you think?"

"Not really. I think I've maxed out my trouble meter. Nothing more my folks can do that they haven't done already."

But the moment had passed. We spent the rest of the free period with Amy catching me up on what I'd missed in our classes.

That afternoon, it was clear my teachers were surprised to see me. Adam must have told them to not expect me "until further notice" or something.

When the final bell rang, I ran into Zach as he was coming to get my World History homework.

"Dude, what are you doing here?" he asked.

"I go to school here," I said, feigning confusion.

"Come on, man, you know what I mean. Did you apologize to Dad or something?"

"Nope. Just decided to come to school."

"Oh man, Dad's gonna flip. I can't decide whether I want to be there to watch or whether I should get out of the state."

I smacked the back of his head. "Haha, very funny."

"Seriously, Rudy. Dad's gonna be livid. Are you sure you know what you're doing?"

I took a breath. "Honestly, man, I don't know. I just don't care anymore. I don't owe him anything. Has he told you what all of this is about?"

"Uh-uh," he said, shaking his head.

"I don't wanna drag you into it. It's not your fight. I just don't think Dad and I have much to say to each other any more. We can ignore each other until graduation, and that'll be that."

Zach gave a somber nod. "Well, good luck, man. I think I'm gonna find Ben and see if I can hang at his place tonight."

I chuckled. "Probably not a bad idea. And hey, thanks for picking up my homework these last few days. Really, I appreciate it."

"Sure thing. See you later?"

"Yeah."

I stopped by a store on the way home and picked up a cheap prepaid phone, then texted Sim and Amy my new number. Adam could take away my old phone, but he had no right to touch this one. It felt good being connected again.

Without Otis to get me around, it took a solid hour to walk home, and it was nearly 5:00 by the time I turned on to the street. Adam's car was in the drive, and I steeled myself for the encounter I knew was coming.

Not surprisingly, both he and Mom were sitting in the living room, an exact replica of the scene from Monday night.

"Déjà vu," I said, closing the door.

"You were grounded."

I set my backpack on the ground, but stayed standing. "Dispensing with the pleasantries? Okay. Yeah, I was grounded. But I'm done with that now."

Adam stood, apparently uncomfortable with me holding the authoritative position.

"You don't get to decide that. I told you that you would remain in your room until you repented, and that's exactly what's going to happen."

"No."

Adam's face turned red. I forced myself to stand firm, but it wasn't easy.

"*Go to your room!*"

"No," I said again, forcing my voice to remain steady. This was the moment I wasn't sure about. Would Adam try to force the issue physically? Or would he just let it go?

The red faded from his face, and it took on a pained look. Almost like I'd slapped him.

"I don't understand. We raised you to respect authority. To honor your parents. I don't understand why you've chosen to reject everything we've worked to instill in you, but I won't support it. You have a place here until you graduate. The day after that, you will no longer be welcome in this home."

"Fair enough."

That pained look again. He hadn't expected me to respond to his ultimatum with such nonchalance. Maybe he thought I'd break down at the thought of being kicked out.

It was surprising that he hadn't expected that I'd actually want to leave.

I grabbed my backpack and headed for the bedroom, happy to go there as long as it was my choice rather than his mandate.

It was done. Just seven more months, and I'd be gone.

16

With everything out in the open, life at home got awkward fast. Mom and Adam were both hurt, and neither seemed to know what to say. Any conversation we had over the weekend was stilted and short-lived.

I felt bad for Zach. In light of my recent rebellion, Adam had cracked down on Zach's social activity. He demanded an hour by hour accounting of where Zach was, what he was doing, and who he was doing it with. I'd tried to apologize for putting him in that position, but Zach blew it off. "It's just Dad being Dad. No big deal."

I wished I could let it all roll off my shoulders like that.

The first Sunday in November dawned crisp and cool. Octobers here border on the schizophrenic. Leaves start changing colors, but the weather can't decide between cooling off or replaying August. By November, though, things start trending colder. The sun was shining, but there was a bite to the air that necessitated a jacket.

Not sure why I decided to go to church. Pastor B's sermons provided no answers, and I wasn't playing the piano anymore. Dad had called the church and told them that I "would be unable to perform." Who knows what details he gave them, but I didn't really care. And, silver lining, I no longer had to get up early on Saturday.

That alone *almost* made everything that had happened worthwhile.

Amy definitely made it all worth it. And the biggest advantage to my new reality was that I no longer had to hide how I felt about her. Amy told her mom about us over the weekend, part of a renewed effort to be open and give her mom a chance to hear her out. She took it pretty well, though I guess she had a bit of a hang up about my apparent "rebellious streak." I made a mental note to be as respectful as I could around Claire moving forward.

We were now free to be a couple in public. We sat next to each other in church, her hand in mine. Even if I couldn't think of any other reason to be at church now, Amy being there was reason enough.

When service let out, I left with Amy. She dropped her mom off at home, then drove us over to the Mile-Hi Diner. As we sat down with burgers and milkshakes, she asked, "So, what now?"

"Well, now I thought I'd eat this cheeseburger."

She threw a fry at me. "I mean beyond that. Beyond all of this. This has to change your plans. What are you going to do about college?"

I shrugged. "I've been debating college for a while now anyway, the way tuition keeps rising…I've never been able to settle on what I want to study, anyway."

Amy took a swig from her milkshake. "So, if no college, then what?"

I took a bite from my cheeseburger to buy some time to think about my answer. I'd been thinking about it quite a bit since Friday night, but I still wasn't sure what I would do. Swallowing, I said, "I guess I don't really know yet. I've thought about just finding a part-time job somewhere and starting to build up a base of piano students. There's good money in that if you can find enough people. I also thought about going to trade school for welding or air traffic control or something like that. Big need for both those things, and I hear they pay well."

"Where would you live?"

I could tell what she was getting at. "Guess that depends. I can live anywhere while doing any of those things. I guess the real question is, what are you doing after graduation?"

Amy blushed. "I thought I knew. I used to think I'd study marine biology or something like that. But ever since Dad died…" She let that hang in the air. "I don't know. I don't think I want to spend a lot of time around the water. I'd be thinking about him constantly, and it's already hard enough to deal with. I might become a dental assistant or something."

I raised an eyebrow. "Dental assistant? Really?"

"I like teeth," she said, shrugging. "I think they're interesting."

"Okay. Wow. Wouldn't have pegged that."

"Oh, the things you don't know, Nathan Rudolph."

I stopped eating and looked at her. "I want to find out."

"What do you mean?"

I reached out and took her hand. "Whatever happens after graduation I want to be wherever you are. I want to keep learning all those things about you that I don't know yet."

She smiled. "I want that, too."

We went to Belmar Park after lunch. Like a hundred other parks in the Denver area, Belmar has the requisite small lake, several different playgrounds, baseball diamonds, and wide open fields.

For an hour, we just walked. Sometimes talking, sometimes not, always with her hand in mine. It had warmed up a little since the morning, and I left my jacket in the car. The air was still crisp, and the day was beautiful. Most of the trees had started shedding their leaves. They made that crunching noise as we walked.

After an hour or so, we came to a bridge over the lake and stopped. Amy pulled a water bottle out of her purse.

"I think the day calls for a toast."

I looked at her. "Isn't it bad luck to toast with water?"

"Who said anything about water?"

Then I got it.

She retrieved two small paper cups from her purse. It was clear some planning had gone into this. I watched as she poured, not a huge amount, but definitely more than she'd poured out a week ago.

She handed me a cup, then raised hers. "To the future, whatever it may bring."

"The future," I said, "clinking" my paper cup against hers. I threw it back trying to look like an old pro. Despite everything, the idea of drinking still made me a little uneasy. But it made Amy happy, and I wanted nothing more in this world than to make Amy happy.

"Now your turn."

"My turn?" I asked.

"Yeah! I made a toast, now you have to." She retrieved my cup and began refilling both.

"Are you sure about this?"

She rolled her eyes and handed me the cup. "Stop worrying. This isn't enough to really make me tipsy. I'm still good to drive. You might get a little buzz, but not enough to really be drunk. Trust me."

I looked at the cup in my hand, still uneasy. But...

Lifting the cup, I said, "To Amy Davidson, the girl I trust more than anyone on this planet."

She giggled. "To me." We "clinked" and threw back our paper cups once more.

Amy stowed the water bottle, and we pitched the cups into a small trash can at the end of the bridge. We stood there leaning against the rail. Amy looked out across the water. I looked at her. My whole life had come undone in the course of a single semester, but it was all okay. Better, even, than it had ever been. All because of her. She was my whole world now, and I was perfectly happy with that.

"What are you thinking?" she asked, not turning from the water.

"Lots of things," I said. "I'm thinking about how beautiful you look standing there. I'm thinking about how insanely lucky I am to be your boyfriend. More than anything I'm thinking about how much I love you."

She turned then. I couldn't tell if she was blushing, or if it was just the chill of the air lending her cheeks a pinkish tint. She reached up and kissed me. I kissed her back, and lost all track of the world.

It was long dark by the time Amy dropped me off at home. Adam had stopped holding vigil in his recliner. He almost religiously avoided the entire room now, though I suspected it was more me he was avoiding than the space itself. Zach was the only one in sight when I came in the front door, his eyes fixed on a movie.

"Hey, dude," he said, eyes not moving.

"Hey."

And that was it. The beautiful simplicity of filial conversation.

I headed for my room and opened my laptop. Adam had relented to Mom's insistence that I needed a computer of some kind to finish out the school year. Though it was made clear to me that the computer remained their property, they would allow me to continue using it until I graduated.

I opened Xpedition and set it to Stealth Mode. That done, I entered the web address from memory and typed in the login details Mark had provided. A new page loaded with a pretty standard looking forum, one that he'd titled, "The Jazz Room." A couple entries had already been created. There was a brief tutorial on how to use the forum, then

Mark had put another one up Saturday morning.

A New Beginning

Well, here we are. One chapter closed, a new one starting. And I want to say first and foremost, Rudy, don't sweat it. Seriously, it could have happened to any of us, and it was probably inevitable. The CIA, we aren't.

But now that we find ourselves relocated to our new "jazz room," we might as well make the most of it. I think this may turn out to be better than the system we had before. Better anonymity, less chance of getting caught a second time around. And, instead of only being able to meet once a week for an hour or so, we can now discuss our questions and studies in real time.

Just to recap, here's the current version of the List:

1. If God is good and sovereign, then how can evil exist? If He causes evil, can He truly be good?

2. How does election work? Can people choose their eternal destiny, or does God choose for them?

3. How can a good God allow all of the pain and suffering we see in the world?

4. What should life look like for a believer, specifically in regard to a relationship with God and the battle with sin?

I don't have much to add to it yet. With everything going on lately, I haven't been very good about putting the time in to exploring these questions. But I encourage everyone, myself included, to really dig in to 3 and 4. These are great questions, and I'm excited to see what insights our studies yield. Take care!

- Mark

I opened a new Word document and began by offering an apology for everything. Sure, Mark had said not to sweat it, but it was still my fault that everyone had been outed to their parents, and it seemed an apology was the least I could do.

Then I started hammering out a response to question four. I shared what I had found in Romans 7 and I Corinthians 3. I talked about Paul's writings on our sinful nature, and how it seemed that faith in Christ was what brought salvation, then our own efforts after we were saved determined the size of our eternal reward. Just as long as there was faith in Christ and genuine repentance, it seemed that no matter what, we were good as far as eternity was concerned.

Perhaps not the most inspiring of answers, but it had brought me some comfort. Life might prove to be rough. I'd probably be fighting with lust until the day I died, but as long as I kept fighting, repenting, and trusting, then God and I might be okay with each other.

I looked over *The List* again. Question 3 still sat unanswered. The clock on the screen read *12:37a.*

The answer to pain and evil in the world would have to wait at least one more day.

17

It took two solid weeks to feel like I wasn't behind in class anymore. Any time that wasn't spent in class was spent buried in textbooks trying to catch up. College may not be in the picture anymore, but I figured that a solid GPA would at least help with any employment or trade school applications.

Amy and I spent nearly all of our study time together. It had taken the better part of two months, but we could now sit in the same room and manage to focus on something other than each other. It wasn't easy, but we could do it.

With only five weeks left in the semester, we were both forced to stop procrastinating on our term projects for Church History. Friday night, Sim, Amy, and I claimed half of a long table at our neighborhood Starbucks and spread out with books by and about our respective subjects.

Every few pages, I looked up and watched Amy, trying to be as subtle as possible so I wouldn't interrupt her. While she looked as beautiful as ever, I'd recently begun to notice darker circles appearing under her eyes. Darker, yes, because now that I noticed them I realized they'd always been there. I began to wonder if she got enough sleep, if perhaps she struggled with the same kind of insomnia that had plagued so many of my nights.

She caught me watching and winked, smiling. I wanted to kiss her right there, but in the middle of Starbucks with Sim watching…it'd just be awkward for everyone. So I winked, smiled back, and silently cursed the table separating us.

Turning back to my own reading, I sighed. Mr. Wesley was becoming a bigger pain in the neck every time I opened his biography. In the 1730s, he traveled to the newly founded New World colony of Georgia as a missionary. Once there, he tried to apply his style of holiness to the colony. He was rude, unyielding, and even had the colony's only doctor arrested for violating the Sabbath. That ended badly when a poor woman miscarried because the doctor couldn't reach her in time to save the baby.

This was the guy I was supposed to write about. My lousy paper was changing from, "He seemed really committed. I wish I could feel that way," to, "Wow. This guy had way too high an opinion of himself. Seems like someone could have taken him down a peg or two."

"I think I've decided I hate John Wesley," I declared. "First dead guy to hold that honor. How about you guys? Making any progress?"

Sim set his book down. He'd opted to start with a biography on Billy Sunday that was apparently written for kids.

"I guess so," Sim said. "So far, it's pretty much like the notes Ms. Waller handed out. He played baseball, then became a Christian and started working with the YMCA. A neat story, but nothing earth-shattering yet. Not sure what I'll focus on for my paper."

Amy stretched. "Yeah, that's about where I am, too. Though there is one thing about Oswald Chambers that I found interesting."

"Yeah?" I asked.

She nodded. "He struggled with his faith a lot more than I ever knew. Actually, I guess not his faith so much. His belief in God was pretty steady. But he struggled with himself a lot. I guess he felt pretty bad about his own sin. He was smart and a teacher, and people put him up on a pedestal, but it made him feel like a hypocrite."

"No kidding," I said. "Sounds like the complete opposite of Wesley. The guy was kind of a jerk. He acted like he was some upright, holier-than-thou figure, and he had next to no grace for other people's failings. So, while he would probably have put himself on a pedestal, I don't think many other people would have."

Sim sighed. "Sounds like we're making some real progress."

Amy laughed. "Maybe there's more we just haven't gotten to yet. These guys are all still talked about decades or even centuries after they died. Surely they did *something* to warrant that."

I looked at the book in my hands, my finger holding it open where I'd stopped reading. Barely a quarter of the way through the book.

"I don't even want to think about finishing this."

Sim shrugged. "I told you, man, go for an easy one. But,

nooo…Rudy has to pick up the oldest, most mind-numbing book he can find."

I frowned, frustrated, but not really at him. "Well, it made sense at the time. Find a biography written by someone that was actually alive around the same time Wesley was. Just backfired."

"Well, we've still got a little over a month," Amy said. "Maybe just break it up a bit? Read a little each day?"

I thought about that. With over three hundred pages still to go, I wasn't sure whether I'd rather just plow through the thing, or subject myself to a small amount each day. Either way sounded torturous.

"Maybe," I allowed. "But I'm done with this for tonight."

"So, what now?" Sim asked. "We could go back to your place. Play a little CoD?"

"Ugh."

Sim grimaced. "Things still rough at home?"

I leaned back in my chair and stretched, suddenly feeling way older than seventeen. "I don't think things are gonna be okay at home until I can graduate and leave. Dad and I haven't said one word to each other since I told him I was done being grounded."

"What did he ground you for in the first place?"

I looked at Amy. She shrugged. The cat was pretty much out of the bag at this point anyway.

"You know how Amy and I have been hanging out on Tuesday afternoons?"

"I guess. You've been hanging out a lot, so I hadn't really noticed anything specific to Tuesdays."

"Well, Tuesdays have been a little different. We've been meeting with some other kids to discuss questions about God that we didn't feel comfortable asking at home or at church."

"Seriously? You guys were having a Bible study?"

I nodded. "Yeah. We basically swore ourselves to secrecy unless we heard someone else asking similar questions for themselves. Anyway, my dad went through my backpack and found some of my notes. He went ballistic and demanded that I tell him what it was all about, but I refused. He grounded me, and the rest is history."

Sim looked down at his hands. "You didn't think you could trust me?"

"It honestly wasn't that. I just wanted to do right by the other guys. It was a huge opportunity to talk about things that were weighing on my mind, and we all thought it was safest not to tell anyone. I swear it had nothing to do with not trusting you."

Sim didn't respond.

"You mad?" I asked.

He shrugged. "A little hurt, I guess, but I'll get over it. It's actually kinda funny. You got grounded for going to a Bible study. You'd think your dad would be glad about you taking extra time to dig into things. I thought that was, like, his thing, you know?"

I rolled my eyes. "Yeah, except I wasn't doing it on his terms. I couldn't accept his answers. And as far as he's concerned, any answers that aren't his answers are the wrong answers."

"So, to sum this up, you had questions that your dad didn't want to talk about. At least, not in a way that satisfied the questions you had. You tried to find other answers, and he's kicking you out of the house for that?"

I laughed. "That's about it. I think he'd say he's kicking me out for my 'defiant and rebellious attitude', but yeah. It's basically because I can't toe his theological line anymore."

Sim shook his head, the amusement slowly fading from his face. He got lost in a gaze into nowhere, and we all fell silent for a moment.

"This, man," he finally said. "This right here is the kinda thing that makes it so hard for me to buy any of this stuff. Christians can't even agree on what to believe about God. You'd think if God really wanted people to know about him, he would have made it easier. Given you a shorter book or something."

I didn't know what to say. Apparently, Amy didn't either because we both just sat there.

Finally, she asked, "When did you stop believing in God?"

He shrugged, looking at his hands again. I couldn't recall ever seeing him look so ill at ease.

"I don't know," he said. "My parents believe. We go to church on Sundays, but we never talk about it much at home. I grew up believing because they believed. I guess if they'd told me there was a Santa Claus I would have believed that, too. But over the last few years, questions just started piling up. Like this one. If God were real, why wouldn't he just make it easier for people to believe in him? I mean, why wouldn't he at least make it easier for the people who do believe in him to know what to believe *about* him? A guy could go crazy trying to figure it all out!"

I nodded, knowing I couldn't disagree with him. I'd been on the verge of a nervous breakdown over these questions before finding the Cult. Even now, the weight of such questions made me wonder if I'd ever be able to truly *know* God.

"So, how'd you decide to stop believing?" Amy asked.

Sim shook his head and held up his hands, uncertain. "I don't think it was ever that simple. I never felt like I was making a decision to not believe in God so much as I was waking up to the realization that I never really believed in him in the first place. I mean, I probably would have said that I did when I was little, but I never really understood what I was agreeing to. When I grew up enough to understand what it all meant, I just couldn't get my head around it."

"Doesn't the idea of hell scare you?"

"Maybe," Sim admitted. "But it's like everything else. I just have a hard time believing it's really real."

"I don't think I could live in the dark on that," Amy said. "I think it'd drive me crazy until I came to an answer."

Sim ran a hand through his hair. "Yeah, I can understand that. I've just never felt that drive. Maybe God's real, maybe he isn't. Doesn't seem like it's ever going to affect my life one way or another."

Amy fell silent, and I had nothing to add. We sat there for a few minutes, Sim staring absently at nothing at all, Amy fiddling with the corner of her Chambers biography. Me watching both of them.

How was it possible? If God was real, why wasn't there something more that we could say to prove it to Sim, to at least force him to ask these questions for himself? And what was God's game here? I believed He was real, but why did He make it so *hard* for people to believe? Why not just show Himself or offer some other kind of solid evidence for His existence? I could remember from sermons and Sunday school lessons the Bible saying that God didn't want anyone to perish but for everyone to repent. If He really wanted that, why not do more? All He had to do was speak one sentence from heaven right now. Just one, and Sim would believe. He'd have to. How could you not believe when confronted with something like that?

The night had turned awkward. Sim and Amy tried to return their attention to their studies, but it was a lost cause. About ten minutes later, Sim pleaded exhaustion, said "Good night," and left.

I slept in that Saturday, enjoying my newfound freedom to do so. I'd agreed to meet Amy for lunch at 1:00, but the world had no demands on me whatsoever before that.

By the time it became uncomfortable to stay in bed, the clock read *11:14a*. I rolled out of bed, shuffled to the bathroom, and showered. As the water beat down on my head, I couldn't get the previous night's conversation out of my mind. Especially Sim's question about why God didn't make it easier. It was just one more question that cast doubt on God's claims about Himself. Why would a good God make it so easy for someone to go to hell, but so difficult to get to heaven? What did that verse say? Something about the road being wide leading to destruction and many going that way, but a narrow road leads to life and few people find it. What kind of good God sets things up that way?

That old familiar pressure was starting to build up again. I could feel it weighing against my soul, threatening to steal my sanity. I shut off the water, toweled off, threw my clothes on, and powered up the computer. Logging in to the jazz room, I breathed a silent prayer that there would be something new there. The group had been almost dead silent since my post. Contrary to Mark's assumption, it turned out that not having a set meeting time had made everyone lazy. And I needed something, any kind of insight that would answer even one of the questions eating away at me.

My pulse quickened when I saw that Dani had finally responded to my post.

RE: The Life of the Believer

Hi everyone. Rudy, I wanted to reply to one of the points you raised in your post. I went to Romans and read through chapter 7, and I found something surprising. You focused on verse 18: "For I know that good itself does not dwell in me, that is, in **my sinful nature***. For I have the desire to do what is good, but I cannot carry it out." I looked it up, and it looks like that's the wording from the New International Version. We go to a pretty traditional Baptist church, so my family has always used the King James Version, and when I look up the same verse, this is what I found: "For I know that in me (that is, in* **my flesh***,) dwelleth no good thing: for to will is present with me; but how to perform that which is good I find not."*

You made the point that if our very natures were sinful, then of course we could never stop sinning, but the KJV uses the word flesh instead. And listen, I'm not claiming to be some Greek scholar or anything, but I looked it up. Whether we're talking about the KJV or NIV, neither of their source materials have any word or phrase that can be translated as "sinful nature." In both cases, the Greek word is "sarx". It's used all over the place in the New Testament, and every single time it appears in the KJV, it's translated as "flesh." Here's one examples in Luke 24:39, "Behold my hands and my feet, that it is I myself: handle me, and see; for a spirit hath not **flesh** and bones, as ye see me have." That's when Christ was showing himself to his disciples after his resurrection, and the word sarx there is used to describe a physical body.

Then I looked at the other verses in the NIV. That same verse in Luke reads, "Look at my hands and my feet. It is I myself! Touch me and see; a ghost does not have flesh and bones, as you see I have." Even there it's translated as flesh. I don't know why, but only in two verses in Romans 7 did they translate it as sinful nature, and in neither of those cases was there any reason according to the original language for them to do that.

I'm not entirely sure what it means, and I know that I've always been taught that we have a sinful nature. But it looks like there may not be a single verse in the Bible that actually backs that up. Paul says there's no good thing in his flesh, or body. He can want to do good, but it's like his body or the animal part of him is overriding his decisions.

It makes me think of I John 4:4. "Ye are of God, little children, and have overcome them: because greater is he that is in you, than he that is in the world." Maybe without Christ, there's nothing we can do about sin. We're just doomed to lose. But maybe with him we've got something more, a greater power that can help us overcome.

There's obviously still a lot to go through on this, and I look forward to hearing what the rest of you think. Have a good weekend.

- Dani

Well, so much for answering questions. Now I had a whole new batch.

18

Amy pulled into the drive at 1:03. I'd have gone to get her, but Adam's "grace" in letting me stay home and use the computer hadn't extended to Otis. He'd confiscated the key, and it was pretty clear I wasn't ever getting it back.

"Hey," she said as I opened the passenger door.

"Hi," I replied. She seemed off, but I wasn't sure why. I searched her face for any sign of trouble, but she was wearing sunglasses with big lenses, the kind only girls can pull off. They obscured enough of her face to prevent giving anything away.

"How was your morning?" I prodded.

"Meh." She sounded exhausted, and thoroughly out of character.

"What's wrong?"

"Oh, it's nothing. Just woke up with a bit of a headache this morning. No big deal."

I wasn't sure I bought it, but her tone and body language suggested that this was not a good time to press.

"Where do you want to go for lunch?" she asked, her voice taking on a little more of her naturally upbeat tone.

I shook my head. "I don't know. I missed breakfast, so make it somewhere cheap with large serving sizes."

She laughed, and the tension eased. We settled on Denny's, about a ten minute drive.

"So, did you see Dani's response to my post?"

Amy nodded. "Yeah, I saw it this morning and glanced through it. I was on my way out the door so I didn't have a lot of time. Strange, though."

"The sin nature thing?"

"Yeah. I've been hearing about our sinful natures for as long as I can remember. I guess I just always assumed it was a given. Like the virgin birth or something."

"I know," I said. "But what if Dani's right? What if we're born *not* with sinful natures, but as blank slates? We end up yielding to the animal or 'flesh' parts of ourselves rather than to what God wants of us. Could she be right that Jesus changes the math once we're saved?"

Amy kept her eyes on the road and didn't say anything for a minute. Then she shook her head. "It doesn't make sense. Paul was saved, right? So what was all that stuff about him wanting to do right, but not being able to? If Jesus changes things and makes us able to win, shouldn't Paul have been able to? I mean, he was an Apostle! If he couldn't do it, even with Jesus's help, what hope is there for people like us?"

Crap. She had me there.

"I don't know," I said. "You have to admit, Sim had a point. Why does all of this have to be so confusing? Why couldn't God have just given us even one book in the Bible that opened with the line, 'Here you go. Simple answers to all of your pressing questions. Enjoy!'"

Amy didn't laugh. She didn't say anything. It was weird. She had a remarkable tolerance for my bad jokes, most of the time offering at least a mercy giggle. But now she looked utterly unamused.

"What are you thinking?" I asked.

She shook her head, as though coming back to the present from wherever her mind had taken her. "Sorry, drifted a little bit. But yeah, you're right. A simple answer book would have been nice."

"Is everything okay? You seem distracted."

"Oh, yeah. I'm just tired. I didn't sleep very well last night, and now this headache today. I just need to get something to eat."

I let it drop again, but I knew there was something she wasn't telling me.

When it comes to food, I'm a simple fellow. On rare occasions, our family has eaten at one of those fancy restaurants with tiny portions and menus with no prices listed, as if they're saying, "If you have to ask, you can't afford it." There's a pretentiousness to the whole set up. Even the food is a bit iffy, sort of echoing the menus. "If you have to ask why this is good, then you don't belong here."

And it's true. I don't belong in those places. I belong in Denny's. Or Pizza Hut. Or McDonald's. I couldn't care less what other people thought was good or bad food. These places all tasted just fine to me. And the most critical thing they all had in common?

They're dirt cheap.

As we walked in the door, I remembered Tim Allen's line from *The Santa Clause*. "Everybody likes Denny's. It's an American institution!"

Couldn't agree more, Tim.

We took our seats and started browsing the menus. One of my favorite things about restaurants like Denny's is that breakfast is available no matter what time you come in. I wanted pancakes, and lots of them.

After finding what I was looking for, I looked up to ask what Amy was going to get. She had taken off her big-lens sunglasses, and I froze.

I could see now why she'd chosen those particular shades. The extra makeup she'd applied that morning couldn't completely conceal how red and puffy her eyes were, or the utter exhaustion they betrayed.

She looked up and caught me staring. I guess my expression gave me away.

She gave a mirthless, half-smile. "That bad, huh?"

"What happened?"

She shook her head and shrugged. "I don't know. I think maybe Sim's questions got to me more than I expected. Didn't sleep much."

We were interrupted then by a young waitress carrying a pot of coffee. I took 66.6% of a cup, but Amy declined. The girl took our orders, and retreated to the kitchen.

As I started filling the cup's remaining space with cream

and sugar, I asked, "You think he might be right? That maybe the complicated nature of all this stuff is actually evidence against it? Against God?"

"Maybe," she admitted. "But maybe not. Even with the questions, evolution still doesn't add up. Beyond any question of evidence or things moving from order to entropy, or anything like that, it just feels wrong."

I made a mental note to find out what entropy was.

Amy continued, "But it does make it harder to believe in a good God. Not only do we have to accept that God allows bad things to happen, like my dad dying or wars in Africa or rape or disease or any of that stuff…"

She paused there, struggling with what to say next. I'd never seen her like this. Through all of our conversations and all of the questions, she'd always been the stronger of us. The one that had questions, yes, but could still believe through them. I wasn't sure I had the capacity to be the strong one here.

Collecting her thoughts, she said, "But then added to all of that, we're supposed to accept that it's almost impossible to find answers to some pretty basic questions about God. That beyond cursing us to live on this crap-hole of a world with death and disease and misery, we have a razor-slim chance of even reaching the one thing that can supposedly save us. And then what? Then we still deal with death and disease and misery, and based on Paul's experience, it doesn't seem like anything ever gets any better!"

I didn't know what to say. The fear that had been playing at the corners of my mind swelled. I knew that I didn't have an answer, and despite our work with the Cult, I wasn't convinced that anyone did.

She must have seen how dejected I felt. "I'm sorry," she said. "Really, I probably just didn't get enough sleep last night. Makes things feel bleaker than they are. But it's days like today that I think maybe Daisy was right. Maybe it's better to just be an ignorant little fool."

I nodded, understanding at least a little how she felt. Still, she'd encouraged me more times than I could count, and I figured it was my turn.

"You never know. We still haven't really gotten to dig into your question yet. Maybe there's something we just haven't found that'll help explain all of this."

"You really think so?" she asked.

"It's a big book. So, yeah. It's possible."

The waitress returned with our food, and the conversation gave way to more pressing concerns.

The afternoon was perfect. Fifty degrees and sunny, with just the faintest breeze. After lunch, Amy drove over to Belmar Park, which had quickly become one of our favorite spots.

We walked around for hours, avoiding all theological topics and instead focusing on each other. We talked about the future, about what we'd do after graduation, whether we'd stay in Colorado or move elsewhere. I'd always wanted to at least see a beach, and living near one sounded kinda fun. Amy agreed, but I could tell that her mom being here would prove a big hindrance to ever moving out of state.

Maybe a new town at least. Fort Collins to the north, Colorado Springs to the south. They were both close. We could move away and get some distance from everyone else's expectations, but she'd still be close enough to see her mom whenever she wanted.

"You realize you're kinda skipping a big piece of the puzzle, right?" Amy asked. Now that we'd moved away from questions we couldn't answer, her playful humor had returned.

"Yeah?"

She nodded. "Yeah. How are we going to move anywhere? Are we going to find separate apartments or something."

"Maybe. I guess there's only a few different options there."

"Yeah? What are the others?"

She knew. She had to. But I wasn't sure how to bring it up. We'd never really talked about where the relationship was going. But I knew we both believed sex before marriage would be wrong. Which meant living together without getting married was out of the question.

But it was crazy, right? I mean, we'd know each other for how long? Three months? People these days dated for years before getting married. Was I insane for even entertaining the notion? *At seventeen?*

Probably. But what was sanity's virtue?

I stopped walking and turned to face her, taking her hands in mine.

"I think you know what the other options are," I said. "But I need you to tell me if you think that's totally crazy."

She smiled, that playful one she used when delighting in my torment. "Depends on what you're asking."

I laughed, feeling suddenly awkward. "I guess I'm asking if you could imagine, you know, maybe after graduation... marrying me?"

"Nathan Rudolph, are you proposing to me?"

I shrugged. "I don't know. I don't really want to like this, but it's hard to plan for the future without knowing if there is a future. I guess I'm asking if you think, if I were to propose in a few months, if you think you might, you know, say yes?"

She tilted her head and said, "Hm. Who knows? I guess you'll just have to wait and see."

It wasn't a yes, but it definitely wasn't a no. I pulled her close and kissed her, reveling in the day, in her being there in my arms.

Maybe it was crazy, thinking about marriage at our age. But it seemed to me that people only waited because they thought they still hadn't found the person they wanted to spend their lives with. I had, so why wait?

I couldn't think of a single reason.

Half past midnight, my phone rang. I'd gone to bed about an hour earlier, and when I woke up it took a minute to remember what planet I was on and another to find my phone after I knocked it to the floor and it bounced under the bed. By the time I found it, the phone had stopped ringing.

I looked at the screen.

Missed Call: Amy - 12:34a

I hit redial and started pacing my room while it rang. We'd spent the whole afternoon and most of the evening together. Why would she be calling now?

The call was answered on the second ring.

"Rudy?"

"Mrs. Davidson?" I asked, suddenly concerned. "Is everything okay?"

"Not exactly. I'm sorry to bother you so late, but could you come over?"

"Sure," I said, looking around for my shirt and socks. "What's going on?"

"I'll explain when you get here. Thanks." The line went dead.

Strange. Mrs. D had never called me before. And she didn't sound mad. More distracted than anything, and maybe a little worried. I threw on my clothes as fast as I could and moved slowly into the living room. It'd be a half hour jog to their house, and I didn't love the notion of arriving totally out of breath. I stole the key to Otis from a ring on the refrigerator and left the house as quietly as I could. Adam might hear the car turn on, but there wasn't a whole lot he could do to stop me by that point.

I drove flirting with the line between speeding and safety. Last thing I needed at this point was a traffic ticket, but curiosity and concern won out.

It was nearly 1:00 in the morning by the time I arrived.

Knocking on the door, I breathed a silent prayer that everything was all right.

Mrs. Davidson opened the door, smiled, and ushered me inside. Amy was nowhere to be seen.

But I could hear her. I guessed she was in her room, her door and the walls muffling the alternating sounds of crying and yelling.

"What's going on?" I asked, suddenly terrified.

Mrs. D looked like she'd been crying. "I was hoping you could tell me. She came home tonight, and we talked for a little while. I went to bed around ten, then woke up about an hour ago to basically the same thing you're hearing now. I tried to get in, but she locked the door and won't open it."

It made no sense. Things had been fine when I'd dropped her off. Better than fine. We'd had a great day.

Or so I'd thought.

"So, why'd you call me?"

She smiled through the sadness. "I know how she feels about you, Rudy. I'm hoping that maybe she'll let you in."

I nodded, getting it now. Steeling myself for whatever was about to happen, I moved to Amy's door and knocked.

"Amy?" I called out. "It's Rudy. Can you let me in?"

The sounds on the other side of the door faded to a rustling as she moved around. It was a minute or so before I heard her at the door. There was the sound of a latch turning, and the door opened.

I tried to keep the shock out of my expression, but it wasn't easy. The lights were off in her room, so it took my eyes a minute to adjust to what I was seeing. Amy was a mess. Her normally straight brown hair was a tangled web, and the room itself was a disaster. It looked like she'd taken all of the contents of her desk, dresser, and closet and thrown them into a haphazard pile on the floor. The only thing still sitting on her desk was a three-quarters empty bottle of vodka and a glass.

And based on the smell of her breath, the bottle had been way more full at the start of the evening.

"Amy…"

"Hi, Rudy," she said, directly.

"What's, uh…what's going on?"

"Oh, my room needed a MAKEOVER!" She said the last word so loudly, I cringed. "So, I'm just moving everything around."

"At one in the morning?" I asked.

By now Mrs. D had stepped in the doorframe behind me and was surveying the scene. I could only imagine if Adam had walked in on me in such a state. He would…I couldn't even imagine, but it wouldn't be pretty.

"Seemed like a good time," Amy said, nudging a shoe around with her foot. "Not like I was doing anything else."

I stepped over to her dresser and picked up the bottle. "And this?"

"Oh, please. You're going to judge *me* now? I was just feeling a little tense. Needed something to take the edge off."

I looked at her, then at the bottle, holding it up and giving it a little swirl for effect. "Big edge."

Amy stood up from the bed and grabbed the bottle. "So what if it is?" Disregarding the glass, she tipped the bottle and took two big gulps from it. Trying to sit back down, she stumbled and fell backwards. The bottle hit the floor, remaining intact thanks to the two sweaters and blue jeans cushioning its fall. The remaining contents poured onto the carpet.

Amy pulled herself into a sitting position against the bed and drew her legs up to her chest. Slowly, I moved over to the bed and sat down next to her on the floor. She laid her head on my shoulder, but I couldn't tell if it was due to affection or exhaustion.

Then she burst into tears.

The previous afternoon couldn't have seemed any further away. Just hours earlier we were perfectly happy, even talking about getting married. Now I was sitting on her bedroom floor in the middle of the night wondering if I really knew Amelia Davidson at all.

"Why can't I get it together?" she asked to no one in particular. "Why am I such a screw-up?"

I looked at her, wishing I could see her eyes rather than just the top of her head. "What are you talking about?"

"Why can't I just believe everything? I have all these questions and feel so tense I just want to explode."

I lifted my arm up and around her, and she leaned into me.

"I didn't mean to get drunk. It just kinda happened."

The circles under her eyes at lunch played in my memory. "This isn't the first time, is it?" I asked.

She shook her head softly and started crying again.

What was happening? I thought about things I'd heard in health class at school, that something like one in ten people is an alcoholic. It had never for a second entered my mind that Amy might be the one. I silently cursed myself for whatever role I'd played in contributing to this.

"Why would God want anything to do with me?" she asked through the tears.

Mrs. D had been standing in the doorway silent through all of this. It was amazing how calm she seemed. Now she crossed the room and gently kneeled down in front of Amy.

"He wants you for the same reason I do," she said. "Because you're my daughter, and I love you."

Amy looked up at her mom for a long moment. Then she almost jumped forward, hugging her mom as though clinging to life itself, and crying even harder.

"I'm so sorry, Mom. I'm so, so sorry…"

After a long minute like that, Mrs. D looked and me and I mouthed, "I just gonna…" and gestured toward the door.

She nodded once and mouthed back, "Thank you."

I nodded, and gave a slight smile as I retreated silently from the room.

19

I didn't get home until almost 2:30. To my surprise, Adam wasn't waiting in the living room to confront me. I set the key on the kitchen table and wrote out a brief note explaining why I'd taken the car. It wasn't exactly an apology, but it was close. I also told him not to wait for me when they left for church in the morning.

Sleep hit hard and fast. As expected, I didn't wake up in time for church. By the time consciousness finally returned, the clock read *1:28p*.

"Ugh..." I groaned, forcing myself to roll out of bed. I picked up my phone and clicked on the front display.

3 Missed Texts

I opened the phone and saw that they were all from Amy.

11:36a - hey rudy im so sorry about last night. i didnt want u to see me like that but i really appreciate u coming. ive never felt so tense as i did last night and it r

11:37a - eally helped having u there. im gonna take today and just stay home. mom and I have a lot we need to talk about and ive got homework stuff. Ill catch up with u

11:39a - tomorrow at school. thanks again for being there for me. i luv u!

As little as tone can be trusted in text messages, she sounded better. I'd been worried for her and praying for her the whole drive home, and it was comforting to see that she was doing better.

Mrs. D's response from the previous night kept playing in my head. No anger, no condemnation. But no condoning of anything either. Just unconditional forgiveness that said, "I'm here, and I'm with you." An odd mixture of jealousy and gratefulness welled in my chest. Jealousy that I got stuck with Adam when Amy had Claire. But gratefulness that... Amy had Claire. Especially now.

I laid back on my pillow and let my thoughts wander. By the time the sound of voices in the living room snapped me back to reality, it was almost 3:00.

With the morning gone and the afternoon already half spent, I decided against calling Sim and started working through some homework of my own. There was barely a month left in the term, and it was crunch time. Sure, one could wait until the week before finals to start buckling down, but by then you were racing against time, and I hated that feeling. Better to get ahead of the game than try to catch up.

I ate dinner with the family that night and was pleasantly surprised that things were almost normal. Adam didn't berate me for taking Otis the night before. He didn't even mention it. Mom filled me in on what I missed at church (spoiler alert: not much), and Zach raved about the advance footage for some new *Star Wars* game that was due out soon. Adam kept mostly to himself.

Just like old times.

Monday dawned cold and rainy. Since October's early snow, the weather had settled into a cycle of beautiful fall days interspersed with an impatient winter anxious to take center stage. It wasn't cold enough for snow, which would have at least had its charms. Just cold and wet.

With Otis now unavailable, Sim had started picking me up again. We hadn't talked since Friday night at Starbucks, but I figured there wasn't much to say. He'd made his position on God pretty clear, and for the moment at least, I didn't have any answers.

So we shot the breeze, almost like normal. He was raving about a new *Star Wars* trailer that had just dropped online. I was letting him rave.

Okay, I thought it was awesome, too.

So we both raved about the trailer and gave the perfunctory mocking of Jar Jar Binks and Hayden Christensen and the terrible misadventure that had been the entire prequel trilogy.

By the time we got to school and shambled into Algebra

II, things felt pretty good between us. We kept chatting about everything and nothing until the bell rang, and it wasn't until we hit the D's in attendance that I realized Amy's desk was empty.

I tried to subtly remove my phone from my pocket and check for text messages while Mr. Reynolds had his head down looking at the roster.

No missed calls. No missed texts.

It was probably just the hangover. Having no experience of my own, I didn't really know how long they lasted, but based on her condition when I left on Sunday morning, it seemed like she might be in for a doozy of a recovery.

Class wore on, somewhat more boring than usual without her there to help me while away the hour passing sarcastic notes back and forth. AmLit passed much the same, then I spent free period dozing alone in the library. When I rose to head to lunch, I fired off a quick text. *hey, missing you at school. algebra 2 was a snore, and amlit was about the same. hope you're feeling all right!*

Sim caught up with me in the cafeteria line, and we both settled in to enjoy the wonders of tater tots and salisbury steak.

"Listen," Sim said, working his way through his third bite of the barely edible meat. "I'm sorry about Friday."

"Okay..." I said. "Why?"

He shrugged. "I know you believe in God and all that. I'd hate to make that harder for you."

I smiled. "Thanks, man. But you got nothing to worry about. God and I have enough problems with each other right now, and you're not the cause of any of them."

Sim nodded. "How are things going with this Cult of yours?"

"Okay, I guess. We've relocated to an online forum, and it's okay. Not quite the same, though."

"Yeah," he said, nodding. "I'd imagine the clandestine meetings in the jazz room were a little more engaging."

"It did add a layer of drama, I'll give it that. Seems like since we stopped meeting there people haven't taken the questions as seriously. Just hasn't been much follow-through with the new format."

Sim nodded, but didn't respond. He picked at a tot, peeling pieces from it one at a time. In all the years we'd been friends, he'd never been as pensive as I'd seen him this term.

"What are you thinking?" I prodded.

"I guess I'm thinking that I'm impressed," he said, dropping what remained of the tot. "Even with all of the questions and whatever, you're still able to believe. It seems…I don't know. But I'm impressed."

I laughed, and a bit louder than I meant to. "Sorry, man, but that's kinda funny. Believe me, there's nothing impressive about it. It's more of a curse than anything else. I just can't buy evolution. If I could, then maybe all of this would be easier. I could join you under the agnostic banner. But I can't. That leaves God, and near as I can tell, the Bible's God is the closest thing to a God that actually makes sense in the real world. I believe it not because I want to, or because I have some really strong faith. I just don't really have much choice."

Sim smiled. No mockery, no jokes. Just a gentle, honest

smile.

"Well, if you ever find those answers you're looking for, you'll have to let me know."

I nodded. "Will do."

When school let out, the rain had stopped. The clouds still lingered heavy and low, and it seemed like a good afternoon for slaying zombies.

Amy still hadn't replied to my text, but I figured if she was still recovering, she might be trying to sleep the day away. I made a mental note to call her after dinner.

As Sim rounded the corner onto my street, he said, "Looks like you guys have company."

He was right. A sedan I didn't recognize sat in the drive behind Otis.

Sim dropped me at the curb, and I pulled my jacket tight against the brisk November wind as the rain started up again. I hate the summer heat, but I suddenly missed July.

As soon as I came in the front door, I saw Adam sitting in his chair. Mom was right next to him in hers, holding his hand. On the couch across from them sat Pastor B.

So, this was why Adam waited to say anything about my taking Otis that night. And now they've looped the good Pastor into our little family drama.

"So, what is it this time?" I said, not bothering to conceal my frustration.

"Nathan, honey. Please come sit down," Mom said. It was a request, not a demand. "We need to talk to you."

Something was wrong. She was tense, but not angry tense. I looked at each of them again. Adam wasn't meeting my eyes, and Pastor B sat staring at the cover of the Bible in his hands. Mom looked off.

Then it hit me. She'd been crying.

"What's going on?" I asked, suddenly panicked. "Where's Zach? Is he okay?"

Mom started crying again, and Dad still couldn't look at me.

Yeah, in light of whatever was happening, he was Dad again. For now.

Pastor B finally turned to look at me, and I braced for what I knew was coming.

"Nathan, Zach's fine. As I understand, he's with a friend right now."

I gasped, relieved. But my relief vanished almost as fast as it had appeared. Zach might be okay, but Mom wasn't crying for nothing.

"Pastor, why are you here?" I asked, terrified of the answer.

"Nathan, why don't you come sit down with us?"

"I think I'm good standing," I said, my growing panic overriding any courtesy. "And I'd really appreciate it if someone could tell me what the heck is happening right now."

Pastor B looked down at his Bible again. After a moment, he turned back to me, and said, "There was a car accident this morning. Mrs. Davidson was driving daughter to school when a car ran a red light. I guess the road was wet from the rain and they couldn't stop in time.

Mrs. Davidson had just pulled out into the intersection when the car hit the passenger side."

He stopped, and my heart stopped with him.

"Nathan, I'm so sorry. Amy was killed instantly."

I couldn't move. Couldn't speak. My heart flailed about searching for the right emotion.

It landed on despair.

"No…" I whispered, praying this was all some horrible joke Dad had cooked up to get back at me for everything.

"I'm so sorry," Pastor B said again. "Nathan, please. Would you allow me to pray with you?"

"What?" I asked, tears starting to cloud my vision. "You want to pray? What's that gonna do now?"

He seemed stunned. I'd always been the good Christian boy. He must have expected that I'd at least put up a good front. Stand strong against the storm.

But I had no strength left. The truth had been slow in making its impression at first, but now it was making up for lost time. Amy was gone. *Gone*. I would never see her again. Everything we'd planned and promised and…it was all slipping away like water through my fingers, and I couldn't stop it.

Tears started coming, and I couldn't stop them either. Pastor B stood up from the couch and stepped over, reaching up a hand to place on my shoulder.

But something in me revolted. I jerked away from his touch, livid.

"What are you doing?" I demanded.

"I…I'm sorry, Nathan," he said. "I just want to be here for you. God's here for you, too. As much as this hurts right now, we have to remember that he has a plan in all of this."

No. No, you didn't…

"A plan? *A plan!?* You think this was all part of God's *plan?*" A distant part of me knew that I was yelling at a pastor, but I was light years beyond caring.

I laughed, a mirthless, sickening chuckle through the tears. "So, let me get this straight. God, in his infinite wisdom, decided it was part of his eternal plan to bring Amy here, let me fall in love with her, plan a future with her, and then killed her? That about sum it up?"

The man looked like I'd slapped him. "We can't know his plan, Nathan. We…we just have to trust him."

"Trust him? You've gotta be *freaking kidding me!*"

I was practically screaming now.

"No! No, she's gone!" My voice cracked as the tears started coming again. The room swam around me. "She's gone, and if you're right, if he took her…I don't want anything to do with him. I hate him. Do you hear me? *I HATE him!*"

Dad stood up, looking at me for the first time since I'd come through the front door. "Nathan…"

"No! I don't wanna hear it! I don't wanna hear about how I'm blaspheming God or whatever you're thinking right now. You think I care? She's dead, and he either let it happen or *caused* it to happen. How can you worship a God like that? How can you even *believe* in a God like that?"

Mom stood, too. "Nathan, please…"

"No…" I choked out. Grief had become a black hole pulling me toward its nexus, and I could feel the house closing in around me.

"No."

I crossed the distance to the front door in three steps, threw it open, and ran into the rain.

20

I ran, and the rain fell.

It probably soaked me through in the first couple of minutes, but I didn't notice.

She's gone.

I ran.

The rain fell.

The homes went past, and streets turned, and I barely registered any of it. The world didn't matter anymore.

Because she's gone.

I kept running.

The rain kept falling.

After I don't know how long, my lungs burning with the heat of a nova, I collapsed in a deserted parking lot behind a defunct gas station. I gasped for air, and wept.

I wept for her, and her life now over.

I wept for us, and our future gone.

I wept for me, alone and undone.

I wept. Minutes passed. Hours. Day ended, and night

came on. And still the rain fell.

It was cold, but I didn't feel cold. The pain and the grief and the rage all hammered together inside of me like an atomic reaction, crowding out all other feeling.

Finally, somehow, the tears stopped. Maybe there's a capacity limit on how many tears one can produce at a time. I didn't feel any better. I doubted I ever would again.

A random neuron fired in my brain suggesting that if I continued to sit here, I might catch pneumonia. I could die.

Good, I thought. *Who cares?*

My life ended when Amy stopped breathing. If she was dead, then I might as well be, too.

A nearby streetlight kept flickering on and off, and I thought about dying. Did she suffer? Pastor B said she was killed instantly, but was she really? In the seconds it took for metal and glass to reduce her angelic form to a broken, lifeless husk, did she have time to register what was happening? Did she feel the car crushing her?

Or was it like the streetlight? On one moment, then off the next.

Wet streets. That's what he said. The streets were wet, and the driver couldn't stop. What had been so important that he'd been driving so fast in the first place? If the roads are wet, you slow down. Everyone knows that! But he didn't. And Amy died.

"We have to remember that He has a plan in all of this…"

I shook my head at the memory. No. He wasn't allowed to plan this. How could he? And even if he didn't plan it, he could have stopped it. Just like Amy's dad.

And again, it all came back to that question. How can a

good God let all of this evil happen?

He couldn't. Not a good God. It was all a cruel joke. We, the rats in a maze, God chasing us with a flamethrower.

The streetlight flickered off again.

"Rudy! *Rudy!!*"

They were looking for me. *Sorry, Rudy's unavailable right now.*

"Rudy, come on, man! Where are you!?"

It was Sim. I wondered who'd called him.

"Rudy!!"

"What!?" I finally yelled.

I heard running footsteps sloshing on the pavement, and Sim's drenched form rounded the corner of the station.

"Dude, do you have any idea how long we've been looking for you?"

I shrugged.

"Well, come on, man. You gotta get outta this rain."

I didn't move.

"Seriously, man. I mean, how long have you been out here? You're gonna get sick."

I shrugged again.

Sim threw up his hands and walked a few steps away. He turned around and looked and me, scratching at his forehead with one hand. Sighing, he walked over beside me and sat down with his back against the station's rear wall.

"I'm sorry, man. I can't even imagine…"

I nodded and sniffed, but didn't say anything.

"So, what's the plan? Sit here until you die of exposure or something?"

More silence from me.

"It's a good plan. Probably would have worked, too. But here's the thing. The second you pass out, I'm calling 911 to come get you. You'll wake up in a hospital surrounded by a bunch of people that won't leave you alone. Call me crazy, but I don't think that's what you want right now."

Rolling my eyes, I turned to look at him.

"We could opt for plan B. Let me take you home. You can get dried off and warmed up, and I'll make sure no one bothers you. Deal?"

My eyes dropped to the ground, the weight of my own exhaustion crashing down like the Hindenburg. I nodded. Bed didn't actually sound all that bad...

I felt his hand on my shoulder. Sim pulled me to my feet, and I let him.

Sim called my mom on the drive home. I guess she'd been the one to call him when I ran out. He gave her our ETA and hung up. Beyond that, we drove in silence.

It felt like I'd run forever, but cars being what they are, we made it home in short order. Faster than I was prepared for. Pastor B's sedan was still in the drive, and for a moment I thought about running again. If I never saw him again it would suit me just fine.

Sim came around and hauled me out of the passenger seat. As we walked in the house, I saw that Zach had come home. After that brief moment of terror that something had happened to him, it was some small comfort to see him sitting there.

Nobody said anything. Mom came over and hugged me, but she kept it brief. Sim ushered me to my room, and closed the door behind me.

Before it latched, he said, "I'm here, man. If there's anything you need in this world, I'm here."

I turned. "Thanks." It came out as a whisper, but he heard and nodded.

Then I was alone.

Alone.

I stripped off my wet clothes and left them piled on the floor. Pulling on a mostly clean pair of shorts, I collapsed on the bed and slept.

Despite my exhaustion, the night passed slowly. I kept seeing her in my dreams. I'd wake up calling out to her, and her absence crashed against me like a tidal wave every time.

Around 5:00 a.m., a sounder sleep finally came. When I woke again, it was past noon. The rain had stopped, and the sun shone.

I had to go to the bathroom, but I didn't want to move. Pastor B might still be in the living room, and if he so much as opened his mouth I knew I would lose it again.

Eventually, nature won out. I don't know why I expected anything different, but when I opened the bedroom door, no one was there. It made sense, I guess. Amy's life had ended, and mine went with her. But the world kept spinning for everyone else.

After the bathroom, my stomach started growling. It

seemed wrong that I should be hungry, that mundane things like food and eating should still matter. But the growling continued, so I went to the kitchen to find something to eat. As I reached for the handle on the refrigerator, I saw that Mom had left a note on the door.

Nathan,

Baby, I'm so sorry. I don't really know what else to say, but I thought you should know a few things. Claire survived the accident, but not by much. I guess the crash shattered one of her legs and caused some head trauma, too. They have her in a medically induced coma right now until the swelling comes down. I'm going to try to stay at the hospital as much as I can. Her sister is there, and I want to be there to wait with her. I feel like it's the least I can do to help.

But if you need anything at all, you can call my cell and I'll come right home. There are leftovers in the fridge if you get hungry.

I love you, Nathan, so very much, and I'm so sorry about all of this.

Mom

Despite the rumblings from my stomach, I left the refrigerator closed and retreated to my room. I pulled the blinds shut, climbed back into bed, and pulled the covers over my head. The world might still be spinning, but I wanted no part of it.

When I woke again, it was dark out, and there was no light coming from under the door. The clock showed it was well after midnight, and everyone must have already gone to bed.

As I laid there waiting for sleep to claim me again, Amy's face was the only show in the theater of my mind. I could almost hear her laugh, and I could almost feel her lips, and I could almost smell her hair…

But it was all out of reach, and I knew I would never again do any of those things.

The tears came again. I clung to my pillow and screamed into it, railing against the universe. Everything she had ever poured into me, her confidence and joy, her life and faith…it all came pouring out now in an unending river of grief.

I don't know when I fell asleep again, but the next time I opened my eyes, it was light out, and someone was knocking at my door. I didn't answer, but the door opened anyway. It was Dad.

"Nathan? Son, are you awake?"

I turned toward the door. "What's up?"

"It's morning. Almost seven. I know this must be hard, but you really should head back to school. Term's almost up, and you don't want to fall behind."

Don't I, now? I rolled back over and faced the wall.

"Nathan…" he started, then seemed to think better of it. Without another word, he turned and left the room, closing the door softly behind him.

School. Like I cared about graduating, or finishing the term, or anything. There was no meaning to any of it now.

Just one more pointless step on the way to an empty life.

I tried to go back to sleep, but it wasn't happening. The growling in my stomach had become a hollow echo. Dragging myself out of bed, I made my way into the kitchen and poured a bowl of Fruit Loops. I tried not to think about her, but that was beyond futile. There was no way to *not* think about her, and trying only made it worse. She consumed my waking hours and haunted my sleeping ones. By the time the spoon clinked against the bottom of an empty bowl, the grief was welling up again. I dropped the bowl in the sink and returned to my room, tears flowing.

They say time heals all wounds. But that's not true. There's no healing the mortal ones. For those, life just seeps out of you until there's nothing left.

Sleep had abandoned me and taken any hope of solace with it. By the time the sun set, my grief had turned to wrath.

Pastor B's words had echoed in my mind ever since they escaped his mouth. *We have to remember that he has a plan in all of this.* He *could* have done something. He *could* have saved her. He *could* have made it not rain. He *could* have made the brakes work better. He *could* have let Mrs. D catch the previous light instead of stopping at that intersection.

The possibilities were endless, and so were the questions. If he could have stopped it so easily, why didn't he? Why condemn me to this living death and Amy to an actual one?

There was no meaning to any of it, and the conclusion

was inevitable. He was a tyrant. And I hated him.

It was dark now. Mom, Dad, and Zach were all at church. 7:00 p.m., every Wednesday night. Old Faithful couldn't be more predictable.

"I hate you. Do you hear me? *I hate you!*" I shouted into the dark of the night, willing him to respond. *Thunder your Almighty wrath from heaven and smite me, you coward!* Or is this all he could do? Deal out arbitrary death and pain from on high without ever giving the creation a chance to challenge him.

Grief and anger warred in my chest until they threatened to rip me apart. I wanted the pain to stop, but it continued on its inexorable path.

Then it occurred to me. What worked for Amy could work for me, too. And I was no longer burdened by any sense of guilt or duty.

Getting drunk was suddenly all I wanted.

Mom and Dad have always had something on hand. Wine, typically, and Dad normally has beer in the fridge. But I knew I needed something stronger. They keep the harder stuff in the kitchen, in the cabinet above the stove. Dad doesn't drink it often, mostly just when Grandpa comes over and they share a whisky.

I went into the kitchen and opened the cabinet. There sat the familiar bottle, still three-quarters full.

I took it, forgoing a glass. I wouldn't need one.

The cap required a little convincing, but it gave. I tipped the bottle back, the amber liquid burning my throat as it passed. I gagged and coughed a bit, then tilted it back again. The bottle was half empty by the time I paused long enough to notice.

For a few minutes, I didn't feel anything. But soon that familiar warmth began to spread, starting in my chest and working its way to my hands and feet. I felt lightheaded and fumbled around trying to lean on the couch. I missed, and fell against the cushions, whisky sloshing onto the furniture. I laughed. I hadn't done that in days, and it felt good. I tried to force the laugh again, but the moment I did, her laugh echoed in my head. Grief's river rose...

...and so did the bottle. I drank again, two gulps. Three. I coughed, spewing it all over the coffee table. Dad wasn't going to be happy. I laughed again at the image of him walking in the door. Just days before, the idea of him finding me in such a state would have been terrifying. Now it was morbidly funny.

"To the future, whatever it may bring..."

More gulps. Everything swimming. *Did I leave a faucet running? How much whisky left? Bottle won't stay still. Some, maybe.*

Tilting again. Burning. Stomach turning. Falling, bottle breaks. Spinning, spinning... Heaving. Ugh...

The puking brought me back to myself, if only just. The room was still spinning, and my head was already starting to pound. It wasn't supposed to be like this. Wasn't I supposed to feel good, or at least numb? I still felt terrible. Her voice, her laugh, her smile...

They won't stop. They'll never stop.

"You did this..." I whispered, holding my head in my hands. "You...took her from me. You don't love me. You never did. It's all pain. Always was, just...waiting to..."

I cried again. But not for her this time. For everything.

For the cosmic sadistic prank that was human existence. For the hopelessness and vanity of it all.

Then the crying was for her again. Memories flooded in unbidden. Her, sitting in this very spot slaughtering me along with the teeming undead. Laughing at my embarrassment. Talking about church. Her dad.

"She believed in you. Wanted to trust you. Her mom... her mom loved her. Showed her that love. And what did you do? You murdered her. Some *Father*."

The words were forced through tears and clenched teeth. My stomach turned, and I vomited again. The living room stank. I stank. It all felt like death.

But the memories wouldn't stop.

I had to get out of there. Too much in the house triggered thoughts of her. I stumbled toward the kitchen, grabbed Otis's keys. Reached twice for the front door latch before finding it on the third try.

The night air was cold, and it felt good against my skin. T-shirt, jeans. *Where are my shoes? Oh, well.*

The key slipped, and a deep groove appeared in Otis's door. I smiled, "Sorry, buddy. Rough night."

Finally getting the door open, I fell into the driver's seat and dropped the keys on the ground. Leaning out to get them, I heaved again, spraying both the drive and the floor of the car. I coughed and forced the key into the ignition. The engine came to life, and I put it in reverse.

Probably shouldn't drive.

"You named your car Otis?"

Have to get out of here. Now.

I peeled out of the driveway and slammed the brakes,

just missing the neighbor's mailbox. I put it in drive and drove down the street, trying to keep Otis in the middle of a road that wouldn't hold still. I turned from one street to another, eventually finding a wider boulevard. Late and cold, not many people out.

"Why would God want anything to do with me?"

More tears. "He didn't. He killed you. You wanted him, so much it caused you so much pain."

I looked at the sky, the city lights reflecting off the low hanging clouds. "You killed her! Wet streets!? It was *you!* Why? Cause she drank? Asked questions? Why did you hate her!?"

The road still rolled, and it was getting harder to see. Lights dimmer. Hills.

"I hate you! I'll hate you forever. Forget what you want. No more Stealth Mode. Whatever I want. Whenever I want!"

Otis was driving himself now. I couldn't see anything.

I screamed, raging at the sky and the so-called God hiding behind it.

My stomach turned again, and then it wasn't my stomach. Otis was turning. Something hit us. Or we hit something. Glass shattered, airbags deployed, and it felt like I was flying.

Then nothing. I was dead.

Finally.

21

Nothing.

Just black, empty. Nothing.

We were wrong. There is no God. No eternity. Just…this.

I felt relieved. Hell would certainly have been my destination if there was a God.

Something's wrong. If there's nothing, why can I still think? I should be nothing, too.

Aaahhhh…

My head screamed. My legs throbbed. It hurt to breathe. I tried to open my eyes, but nothing was working the way it should.

"That's it, Nathan. Wake up. Come on, young man, open your eyes…"

I couldn't tell where the voice was coming from. Everywhere. Nowhere. But it persisted.

"Come on, Nathan. Open your eyes."

I tried again, and they gave a bit. A blinding light flooded in, and I slammed them shut, my head roaring in agony.

"That's right, good. Do you know where you are?"

I'm not sure I know who I am.

"No…" I managed, barely a whisper.

"You're at the Denver Health Medical Center. You were in a car accident. Do you remember?"

Glass, airbags. Flying…

I nodded, and my head roared again. Everything was agony.

"That's a good sign. With head trauma, short term memory can get a little sketchy. That you can remember bodes well for recovery."

That I can remember…

It all came flooding back. The crash, the whisky.

Amy.

"Here, try to to drink this."

A straw found it's way between my lips, and I pulled. Water flooded my mouth, and only then did I realize how thirsty I was. It was pulled away from me before I wanted, and I groaned in complaint.

"That's enough for now," the voice said. I still hadn't seen the source, and the last thing I wanted was to open my eyes again. "Right now, you need rest. I'll be back in a few hours to check on you."

Then he was gone. My head pounded, and every last inch of me ached. But the pillow was soft and…

When I came to, I wasn't alone.

It still hurt to open my eyes, but not as bad as it did

before. Mom was sitting next to my bed reading, and I could hear Dad's voice coming from somewhere nearby. I tried to turn toward the sound when a wave of nausea hit. I coughed, and Mom looked up.

"Adam! He's awake!"

Dad called for a nurse, and a moment later she filed into the room followed by a man I assumed was my doctor.

"Good afternoon, Nathan," he asked. Definitely the same voice from earlier. "Feeling any better?"

I was still squinting against the light. "A bit."

"A bit is excellent," he said, writing something on a sheet of paper no human being would ever see again. "I'm Dr. Gardner. Now that you've had some rest, I need to ask you a few questions. You feel up to that?"

"I guess so."

"That's great," he said, smiling. This fellow was way too perky for an ICU. "Can you tell me what day it is?"

"I don't know," I said. The doctor started writing again. "How long have I been here?"

He looked at his watch. "About eighteen hours now."

I closed my eyes. "It was Wednesday night. Guess that would make it Thursday. Afternoon sometime."

"Bingo! And your full name?"

"Nathan Everett Rudolph."

"Great. How old are you, Nathan?"

"Seventeen."

"Mm-hm," he said, nodding. "That pretty much covers short term memory. Now, let's back it up a bit. Can you tell me what you were doing last Friday night?"

Friday. Starbucks. Sim.

Amy…

I coughed. "I, uh…I was at Starbucks doing homework with some friends."

Dr. Gardner looked at Mom, who nodded. She and Dad had been standing there throughout the questioning, but had yet to say anything.

"That's great," the doctor said, making still more notes. "Your memory seems to be entirely intact."

Stellar, I thought. Couldn't even manage to get amnesia.

"Now, Nathan," he continued. "I know this may be difficult, but I need for you to walk us through as many of the events leading up to the accident as you can. We've given you as full an evaluation as we can, but we need to know what you did before the crash so we can ensure that there's not anything else that we should be looking out for."

I closed my eyes again. It felt like a bad dream, but I knew it had all been real. The hospital room was proof positive of that.

"I, uh…I was having a bad night." Dad had his arm around Mom, and I almost asked them to leave. It was bad enough without having to relive it in front of them. "I guess I felt pretty down, and I didn't want to feel that way anymore. I knew we kept some whisky in a cabinet, so I got it out and started drinking."

Dr. Gardner nodded. "Do you know how much you drank?"

I started shaking my head, then stopped as soon as the room started shaking with it. "Sorry. I think about half the bottle, but I can't be sure. Then I didn't want to be in the house anymore, so I left. Got in the car and started driving."

I left out any mention of my railing at God. "Guess that probably wasn't the smartest move."

The doctor nodded. "Can't disagree with you there. What's the last thing you remember before waking up here?"

"It's pretty fuzzy. There were hills, and the car was at a weird angle. I remember glass everywhere. Then it felt like I was flying. That's it."

He nodded again, making one last notation before setting his clipboard down next to the beeping machines monitoring my vitals.

"Near as we've been able to piece together from what your parents and the paramedics have told us, that's a pretty solid recounting. It looks like you pounded that bottle of whisky pretty fast, and your system rejected it. I guess you vomited most of it?"

I nodded, trying to avoid looking at Mom.

"Well, that probably saved your life." Dr. Gardner pulled up the chart clipped to the end of the bed and flipped through a few pages. "According to our records, when they brought you in you had a blood alcohol level of .26. Now, anything in the mid-.3s carries the risk of death by alcohol poisoning. Judging by the amount of alcohol you consumed, and the amount it sounds like your body rejected...if you hadn't thrown up, you probably wouldn't have even made it to your car, much less our emergency room."

Nobody said anything, but Mom sniffed, and I could tell she was crying.

"Your next bit of good luck came from forgetting to buckle your seat belt. Your car went off the road, clipped a tree, and rolled down an embankment. Rolled a pretty long way based on what the paramedics told me. Sounds like you were thrown from the car when it hit the tree." He picked the file back up and handed me a paper with two grainy pictures of Otis. The wrecked heap was barely recognizable.

"If you'd been strapped in, you'd have been killed for sure. No way a person survives that. So, you got very lucky twice in one night. I want you to understand that. You shouldn't be alive right now."

I almost told him right there that I wished I wasn't. But Mom was still crying, and I couldn't do that to her.

"There are two reasons why I'm telling you all of this," he continued. "First, because I think you should understand just how close you came to killing yourself. Your parents have told me a little bit about what you're going through, and I'm truly sorry about that. But you should know that if you ever do anything like this again, odds are you won't walk away."

He paused, and looked at me, as though trying to gauge whether his warning was sinking in.

"The second reason is that your road back isn't going to be easy. You've got a nasty concussion on top of your lingering hangover. You cracked three ribs, and one of them pierced a lung. The worst of it for the short term is your right leg. From what they could tell, you half-rolled, half-fell down the embankment. Your leg was twisted around, and you suffered multiple compound fractures. We've already completed one surgery on it, and I'm pretty certain you won't lose it. But you are facing at least one more surgery and months of physical therapy before you'll be able to walk on it again."

I swallowed.

He nodded. "I don't want to lie to you; it's gonna be a rough road back to normal. But you're still here, and as long as that's the case you can still make it. But a lot of this is going to be up to you. You're going to have to want to get back up. I've been doing this a long time, and if there's one immutable truth in trauma recovery, it's that the patient decides whether he's going to make it or not. You're going to have to fight for it."

He went on like that for a while, trying to convince me of the importance of my participation in the healing process and whatever. He talked to Mom and Dad about the regimen of meds and therapies that they had me on or would soon have me on. Then he left, sending a nurse in to schedule my next surgery. I looked at the buttons on the bed, focusing on the one Dr. Gardner said led to the morphine drip. I clicked it, and almost immediately felt a warmth spreading. It was a bit like the alcohol. The voices suddenly seemed far away, and sleep claimed me.

I woke to a different room, quiet and dark. They must have moved me out of the ICU while I slept. I supposed that was good news. Or bad. The jury was still out on whether I was glad to be here or disappointed that the crash hadn't just killed me.

In the hum of the machines, I almost missed the sound of a whispered cry. The thought of facing my parents almost physically hurt, so I didn't turn toward the sound. But as I focused my attention, the voice became clearer.

It was Dad.

"Oh, Father," he cried. "I'm so sorry. I don't know where I failed, but it's all gone wrong. Please help me. Please reach Nathan. Be close to him now and in the days to come. Let him feel your presence and your goodness. Show him your love and your mercy, Father. And heal him, Lord, body and soul."

The words were lost for a moment in his tears, and my eyes welled up, too. He sniffed, and sighed.

"Please, Lord…please save my son."

I didn't know what to feel anymore. It was so much easier when I could just hate him. Why waste energy caring what someone thinks about you if you hate them? But he hadn't cared that I took Otis the night Amy needed me. He let me be when I didn't want to go back to school. And now, after I'd stolen his whisky, puked all over his home, and crashed his car…

I expected to wake up to a lecture. A grand "I told you so" that would justify every interference and invasion he'd ever committed.

But not this. The man I'd defied and mocked and screamed at…was praying and weeping for me.

Silent tears rolled down my cheeks. For a long time I lay there crying, listening to the man I'd thought so hard and unmoving do the same.

I've never liked hospitals.

My appendix ruptured when I was thirteen, and I spent a week in the hospital recovering from the operation, the doctors pumping course after course of antibiotics into my system to stave off infection. From the constant midnight vitals checks preventing any meaningful sleep, to the humiliation of being forced to wear a gown with no back, to the meals that could only charitably be referred to as food, the entire experience had been miserable.

This was a thousand times worse. The way they had my leg bandaged and secured, even rolling over was impossible. By the time morning dawned on Friday, I was beyond uncomfortable. And while being confined to the bed meant that I didn't have to worry about the fact that my gown had no back, the bedpan provided a special kind of humiliation all its own.

Mom and Dad were both there when I woke up. I apologized, and considering everything they were both pretty cool. We were all silent for a while after that. I had no idea what to say to them, and they seemed equally uncertain how to approach me. I still didn't want to tell them about my issues with God, and I wondered how long it would be before Dad wanted to talk about that. It was probably coming way sooner than I wanted.

The morning passed with a parade of visitors. Zach. A nurse. Mark and Dani. Another nurse. Sim came by and talked for a while. Then Dr. Gardner came in, chipper as ever, and made more notes on his clipboard. By the time lunch was over, I was wiped out. Despite having slept more in the past week than any week I could remember, I'd never felt so tired in my life.

The room was quiet again when I woke up. Unlike the ICU, this room had a window. From the fading orange light streaming in through the curtains, I guessed it was probably around 4:00 in the afternoon.

"Hi Rudy."

I jumped at the voice and turned toward the front of the room. Mrs. Davidson sat in a wheelchair next to my bed, her leg propped up in a thick cast, one arm in a sling. She looked almost as bad as I did.

"Mrs. Davidson…" I whispered. "What are you doing here?"

She smiled, sadly. "Your mom told me what happened. Everyone's gone home to rest for a while. My sister, your parents…so I thought we might keep each other company."

I gave her a sad smile. "Sorry, Mrs. Davidson. I don't think I'm very good company for anyone these days."

"Call me Claire," she said. "You're practically an adult, and from what I understand, I was very nearly your mother-in-law."

My eyes welled for the millionth time in a week.

"She told you that?" I asked.

There were tears in her eyes, too. She nodded and said, "Yeah, we talked a lot Saturday night and almost all day Sunday. Amy loved you, Rudy. I hope you know how much."

Tears rolled down my cheeks and I made no move to wipe them away.

"I loved her, too."

"I know you did," she said. "And that's one of the reasons I asked them to wheel me down here. You have to know she wouldn't want this for you. It'd break her heart to see you lying there. She'd want you to get on with your life."

I knew I should feel saddened by that, but I just felt drained. "I'm not sure that *I* want to."

Claire tilted her head. "And why is that?"

"She's gone. I was living on autopilot before you guys moved here. She made me want to *live*. Without her I don't know what any of it's for."

"You don't think there's still a purpose to your life? That God might have something planned for you in all of this?"

That familiar rage rose in my chest. No, I didn't, and it was baffling to me that she of all people could ask that.

"How can *you* believe that?" I asked, trying to keep the anger out of my voice. "Your husband, and now Amy, in the space of one year. How can you believe in a God that would do that to them? To you? They didn't do anything wrong, and he killed them."

"Rudy…it's not that simple. And I think you know that."

I blinked. "What do you mean?"

She shifted, looking pained as she did so. "Amy and I talked a lot in the last couple weeks about this Cult of yours. You all were asking some good questions, but it seems like you missed some fundamental points."

"Oh, how so?" I said, sarcasm seeping in.

She acted like she didn't notice. "For starters, there are no innocents. 'For all have sinned and fallen short of the glory of God', and 'the wages of sin is death'. We brought all of this sorrow and pain into the world, Rudy, not God."

"My pastor seems to think he did."

She nodded. "You're talking about sovereignty and free will? Calvinism and Arminianism?"

I still couldn't fully define either Calvinism or Arminianism, but I nodded and said, "Sure."

"Amy mentioned that you'd all spent some time talking about that. I won't pretend I understand how it all works. God is infinite, and we're finite. I'd imagine that the truth is probably more intricate than any of the answers that our theologians and philosophers have managed to produce. But I know this. Man acts, and God acts. Demons act, and angels act. From what I see in the Bible, it all seems to affect the world, and every individual is held responsible for his or her own choices."

"Even if God's forcing those choices on us?" I challenged.

She ignored my question. "Rudy, can I ask you something?"

I shrugged.

"How long have you been mad at God? Did it start before or after Amy died?"

Stunned, I asked, "What does that have to do with anything?"

"More than you probably realize," she said, her voice as calm and gentle as ever. "There are some things that I want you to understand, but you're so angry at God right now that you can't see straight."

She reached over to my bed and pressed the button to signal the nurse. A moment later, one came in.

"Can you take me back to my room please?"

I sat there watching with my mouth open. This wasn't fair. "Why are you leaving?" I demanded.

"Don't worry, I'll be back. But I think you should take a

little time first, and just be with God. See if you can remember when you started being angry at Him. And consider whether you have any right to be."

Before I could come up with a response, she was gone.

And it was just me, my thoughts, and God.

I didn't like anyone assuming they knew or understood how I felt, but I couldn't argue with her.

I was furious with God.

Mostly, it was because of Amy. But as I thought about it, I realized it had started long before. I was angry with him for never answering my questions. For leaving Sim in the dark. For leaving me to fight against lust all on my own.

Going back to my first meeting with Pastor B right before the term started, I couldn't remember a time when I wasn't at least upset with God.

So what? I thought. *Why shouldn't I be angry with him? He could have prevented all of this! Could have taken away the temptation. Could have made the answers easier to find. Could have helped Sim believe. Could have saved Amy. Nothing had to happen like this, and if this is how he operates, then heck yeah I'm angry!*

The confusing thing was why Claire wasn't angry. She had even more right than I did to be livid, but she didn't seem mad. She didn't even seem all that upset. Sad, for sure, but in the middle of her grief she came into my room to try to convince me that…what? Why had she come to see me in the first place? What did she hope to accomplish?

None of it made sense, and I realized Amy had been

right. I wished I could be like *Gatsby's* Daisy. Ignorant. Bliss-fully unaware. Reality weighed heavier than I could handle.

As I tried to sort it all out, Mom and Dad came in with Zach. They'd stopped by the Mile-Hi Diner and brought bacon cheeseburgers. The food smelled incredible. For the first time since I'd woken up in the ICU, I felt famished.

We ate and talked and even laughed a bit. Dad talked about work, Zach talked about school. I didn't say much of anything, and no one pressed me. They seemed to under-stand that I needed some space, and I appreciated it.

They left a little after 8:00, and the grief started crowd-ing in around me. As an old reflex, I almost started praying, but I still didn't want to talk to him. He killed her, and I couldn't get past that.

So, I laid there, alone and spent, wondering what would come next.

What would happen with school, now that I clearly couldn't finish the term?

What would happen with church? Would they expect me to go back?

What would happen after I graduated? Without Amy, it all seemed pointless.

But as I thought about the future, a new realization dawned on me. The future was coming, and I was going to live. I couldn't leave. I couldn't think of a single reason why, but I just knew it. Whatever happened next was going to happen, and I would have to face it.

That thought made me feel more alone than ever.

22

Claire didn't come back that night. Judging by how she'd looked, she was facing a recovery similar to mine. She had to be exhausted.

I passed a restless, medically-complicated night. It was hard to fall asleep, and every time I managed it, a nurse would show up inside of fifteen minutes to check something.

When daylight finally woke me for good, I felt at least as tired as I had the night before. Maybe more so. I wanted to crank up the drugs and let the day go by without me, but one of the nurses must have removed my morphine pump during the night because it wasn't there when I reached for it.

Great...

As if on cue, every injury flared. I pressed the call button, and a nurse came in carrying a pill cup and a glass of water.

"Hurting?" she asked.

"Yeah."

She nodded. "Dr. Gardner had us take you off the morphine last night. We'll start walking you down to weaker and weaker painkillers. Developing a dependency is always a concern when dealing with meds this strong, and we want to get you on gentler stuff as soon as possible."

"Gentler?" I asked. "You mean less effective?"

She smiled. "Oh, I don't know about that. Your body should have naturally calmed down a bit by now, so morphine isn't really necessary. These are Vicodin. Trust me, they'll do the job just fine."

I took the cup from her and looked at the two white pills. It seemed unlikely that they'd quell the pain as well as the morphine had, but whatever was still in my system was wearing off fast. I tossed back the pills and drank the water to wash them down.

"Great," she said. "We'll bring your breakfast by in a little while."

As she left, she had to step to the side to allow another nurse to wheel Claire in. She looked a little better than she had the day before. Maybe she'd already adapted to the midnight interruptions.

"Good morning, Rudy," she said with a smile. "Sleep well?"

I shook my head. "I don't think that's possible here."

"How long are they keeping you?"

"Not sure. I've got a surgery scheduled on my leg this afternoon, so I guess I'm here for at least another day or two."

"You up for talking some more?"

I shrugged. "Would it matter if I weren't?"

"Of course it would," she said. "I won't force it on you, but I imagine if I were in your shoes I'd eventually want to talk to someone."

"Maybe," I said, trying to make it sound as noncommittal as possible. "So, what should we talk about?"

"I thought we'd start with my last question. Were you able to remember when you started being angry with God?"

She had a way of cutting to the point that brought memories of Amy screaming to the surface.

I sighed. "Well, I guess it's been a while. Probably this whole school year, at least."

"Why did it start?"

The room suddenly felt twenty degrees hotter. I didn't want to confess that lust might be the main reason for the gap between me and God.

"I don't know," I said, trying to keep it vague. "Turns out my best friend isn't a Christian. I'd thought he was for years, but I guess he started having questions, and rather than help him answer them, God just let him walk away. I've had my own questions, but God's been silent there, too. Now Amy's gone, and those questions are screaming louder than ever, but God's still dead quiet. So, I guess I'm mad at him for a couple reasons. First, I'm mad at him for existing at all. If he didn't, then I could just be an atheist along with everyone else, and this whole thing would be easier. Second, and this is probably most of it, I'm furious with him for hiding from me. And from Sim. If he's real, and I have to conclude that he is, then why doesn't he reveal himself to people when they really need him? Why doesn't he provide answers to these questions so people like me and Sim and Amy can find a little bit of peace? I suppose that leads to a third reason. Amy was seeking him, trying to understand, trying to find his love. And he killed her in the middle of it. How am I supposed to believe that he's loving when he does something like that?"

Claire nodded. "Makes sense. Can I ask you something else?"

"You just did."

She smiled. "I suppose so. Rudy, if someone could explain all of these things in a way that made sense, would you still have any reason to be angry with God?"

A weird question.

"I'm not sure," I said. "At this point, I kinda doubt that's ever going to happen."

"You mind if I try?"

I shrugged, but didn't say anything.

"Let me start by making sure I understand what you're thinking. You think that if God had just been more clear to you and Sim and Amy, then that would have cleared everything up? You would have all been able to believe in him?"

I nodded.

"And you think that God killed Amy. You think God's responsible for all of the bad things that happen in this world? Right?"

"Seems that way," I said. "Either my pastor's right and God determined everything before it happened, or else everything's just happening on its own and God's letting it. He lets rapists rape and murderers murder and all of it."

She nodded. "And you think that if someone can stop something bad from happening, and they don't, that's as bad as doing it themselves?"

I pursed my lips and nodded. "Yup."

"All right," she said. "Let's start there. Like I said yesterday, I don't claim to know everything about how God works. Guess I'd be God if I did. But from what the Bible tells us, it seems like God and angels and demons and people all make choices and act on them, and that affects the way things move forward."

"And what if my pastor's right?" I interrupted. "What if God is controlling those choices?"

"That's a hard question. Does it *feel* like he's controlling you?"

That surprised me. "What difference does it make what I feel like?"

She smiled. "Well, I wouldn't normally recommend anyone trust their feelings. But indulge me for a minute. Does it feel like God's controlling your actions, or are you the one calling the shots for Nathan Rudolph?"

It didn't take much thought. "I guess it *feels* like I'm in control."

She nodded. "I'd agree with you. It feels like the decisions I make are up to me."

I shook my head. "But how would we even know? I mean, if God wanted us to think we were acting freely, even if we weren't, surely he could set things up that way."

"I'm sure you're right. But why? What on earth does God gain by creating all of this if he's controlling everything?"

I shrugged. "Pastor B says God does things mainly for his own glory."

"So God gets a kick out of a cosmic play that he wrote and is performing for himself? I don't buy it, and I don't think you do either."

She reached into a pouch on the side of her wheelchair and pulled out a Bible. I'd never seen one look so worn.

"There are a few verses I want to read you. The first is Exodus 6:7. God is speaking to Israel and says, 'And I will take you to me for a people, and I will be to you a God: and ye shall know that I am the LORD your God, which bringeth you out from under the burdens of the Egyptians'."

She flipped forward a few pages. "And in Leviticus 26:12, he says, 'And I will walk among you, and will be your God, and ye shall be my people'."

More flipping. "Then we come to Jeremiah 30:22. 'And ye shall be my people, and I will be your God.' Notice a theme?"

"He'll be their God, they'll be his people."

"Yeah," she said, nodding. "There's similar language in the New Testament. In I Peter 2, Peter writes, 'But you are a chosen race, a royal priesthood, a holy nation, a people for God's own possession, so that you may proclaim the excellencies of him who has called you out of darkness into his marvelous light; for you once were not a people, but now you are the people of God.

"That theme runs throughout the entire Bible. From the creation of Adam and Eve, to God calling Abram to leave his family and his homeland, to Israel being liberated from Egypt and brought to the land of Canaan, to Christ dying on the cross and the disciples going forth in the world to preach. From the beginning, God has been focused on getting a people for himself."

"But...why?" I asked. "He's God. Why not just create Adam and Eve without the tree of the knowledge of good and evil? No chance of sin, no chance of evil, everybody lives happily ever after."

"Exactly," she said, smiling.

I raised an eyebrow.

"You don't see it?"

"See what?" I asked.

"God *could* have done that. He's God; of course he could have created Adam and Eve without that tree. Things would have been peachy. But God doesn't want automatons. You can't force a relationship. People have to *choose* each other. God chose us, while we were yet sinners, and he calls us to choose him right back. The whole Bible is laced with that, with God calling to people to reject sin and choose life. To choose him. If he's controlling their actions, why would he go to such trouble to call everyone to choose him? It wouldn't make any sense."

She sat there for a moment letting her point sink in. I tried to find fault with her logic, but came up empty.

Claire tried to lean forward, and something made her wince. She leaned back and took a breath.

"However God's power works with our choices, one thing seems clear. He's calling, and we have a very real choice about whether or not we're going to answer him."

A nurse wheeled in a floor tray with Claire's breakfast.

With my surgery scheduled for that afternoon, I was only allowed water.

We sat there in relative silence as Claire worked on the bleak spread. Eventually, she asked, "Do you understand?"

I looked at her, uncertain.

"That's why God doesn't stop evil," she said. "If he stopped every bad thing that was going to happen, it'd be exactly the same as if he'd never put a tree in the garden in the first place. For people to be able to choose him, I mean really *choose* him, they have to be able to choose against him. And those choices have to mean something. If they don't, then it's all a charade."

I swallowed. "It doesn't seem right."

"What do you mean?" she asked.

"It's just too much," I said, shaking my head. "Too much death and pain and fear. Doesn't seem worth it."

She nodded. "I understand what you mean. But you're wrong." She must have seen the defensive look on my face because she quickly added, "Don't take it the wrong way. You just haven't lived long enough. You don't have children yet. Imagine it from God's perspective. He's going to create this race, these people that can choose to be the perfect children and enjoy the incredible world he's set before them. Or they can spit in his face and go their own way. It's the same possibility that every parent faces before having a child. Maybe things will go well, maybe they won't. But most people choose to have children anyway."

"Still seems cruel," I insisted. "He had to know how bad it could get if things went wrong."

"He did," she said, picking up the Bible and flipping

through its pages again. "Ephesians 1. 'According as he hath chosen us in him before the foundation of the world, that we should be holy and without blame before him in love.' Then there's Revelation. Chapter 13, verse 8 says, 'And all that dwell upon the earth shall worship him, whose names are not written in the book of life of the Lamb slain from the foundation of the world'."

The same verses I'd studied with the Cult.

She closed the Bible and looked at me. "God knew we might choose wrong. And from the very beginning he had a plan in place to save us if we made the wrong choice. He didn't have to do that. Everyone that's ever lived has had every opportunity to make the right choices and follow God. But in his infinite love, God sent his Son to save us, even though no one deserved it."

The guilt that had taken residence in my soul since Pastor B's sermon at the start of the term now weighed heavy in my chest. I knew she was right. I had chosen to watch porn. *Me.* As nice as it'd be to be able to blame it on someone else, I could have said "No" at any point along the way.

Claire finished her breakfast and pushed the tray out of the way. "Next, you wanted to know why God doesn't just make it easier? Why he doesn't just show himself so everyone could believe, right?"

I nodded.

"Rudy, did it never occur to you that he already has?"

"What do you mean?"

She held up her Bible and let it fall in her lap. "This whole book is full of examples of God revealing himself to the world. And every single time, the vast majority of people rejected him. He created Adam and Eve and walked with them in the Garden. But they chose to listen to the talking snake. He brought Israel out of slavery in Egypt, and before they'd gotten much of anywhere, they decided to make a golden cow their god. The Book of Judges has story after story about God miraculously delivering Israel from one oppressor after another, but Israel always goes right back to rejecting him and doing their own thing. Then Jesus finally comes on the scene. God himself among his creation performing miracle after miracle. And what did the Israelites do? They killed him!

"I can understand wanting to hear from God. Lord knows, I spent my share of nights calling out to heaven for some kind of sign after Trevor died, and I'm sure there'll be more now. But can we really say that if he appeared to us or spoke to us audibly we'd be any more inclined to follow him than the countless people that have heard his voice or seen his power throughout history? Are we really so arrogant as to think that we're any better than they were?"

Shame took its place next to the guilt in my chest.

"It's an innate failing of the human race," she continued. "Doesn't seem to matter how directly God reaches down and acts in our world. We just can't see it when it's happening. Only hindsight ever seems to show us when and where and how God was working."

She fell silent. I watched her run a finger along the spine of her Bible.

"I still don't understand why you're not mad at God," I said. "Maybe God didn't cause the accident. And maybe he can't stop every bad thing from happening without robbing us of free will. But he's intervened before. He's raised people from the dead and healed the sick and all kinds of things. If he could intervene there, why not save Amy? Why did he let her die?"

Claire looked up from the book in her lap, and I could see tears filling her eyes. "I don't know, Rudy. Maybe I'll never know. Why does God rescue one person from harm and not another? I can't say. But I'm not God, and he's entitled to his reasons. He doesn't owe me anything, and he's already given me far more than I ever deserved."

"I'm sorry, Claire," I said. "I just don't get it. It seems like all he's given you is pain."

She reached up and wiped away a tear. "But that's because you don't know the whole story. I wasn't always a Christian, you know. My parents didn't really care much for God when I was growing up. We never went to church, and I thought people that did were silly. Why spend so much time over something that was so clearly a myth? But I started getting myself in trouble toward the end of high school and throughout college. I partied, drank, and slept around. Pretty much did whatever I wanted."

It seemed impossible. For the brief time I'd known her, she'd always seemed so together. A cookie-cutter Christian mom, if perhaps a bit cooler than most.

She took a breath and let it out slowly. "Toward the end of my junior year in college, I had a one-night stand and got pregnant. The guy didn't want anything to do with me, and he wouldn't even admit that he was the father. I was scared of what my parents would think, so I went to a clinic near the school and had an abortion."

I couldn't believe she was telling me this, but I wasn't about to interrupt her for anything.

"I don't know that I can adequately describe the pain of those days. When I left the clinic, I thought I'd feel relieved, but all I felt was emptiness. Over the next few weeks, I slipped into a deep depression. By the end of that semester, I could barely get out of bed. I carried so much guilt and shame over what I'd done, that I didn't think anyone would ever be able to love me again.

"But that's when I met Trevor. He was a cadet at the Coast Guard Academy about a half hour away from where I was going to school, and a mutual friend introduced us. I didn't want to leave my dorm, much less go on a blind date, but my friend was insistent. I still don't fully understand what happened on that date, or why Trevor ever wanted a second one. He was wonderful. Handsome, charming, funny, kind... But I couldn't see past my own pain. And he kept mentioning his faith in one casual way or another. He'd mention his church or how God really blessed him by letting him get accepted to the Academy. I tried to be polite, but I'd never understood people that believed in God. I thought they were weak, which seems ironic now. Anyway, the date ended and he drove me back to my dorm, the perfect gentleman all the way. We said good night, and I expected that to be the end of it."

She smiled through her tears.

"Thankfully, God had other plans. When I woke up the next day, I found a fresh bouquet of flowers outside my room with a card attached. It read, 'Thanks for the date. If you'll let me, I'd like to get to know you better. Dinner tonight?' And he wrote his phone number at the bottom. In the midst of my depression and guilt, I thought it would be fun to test him. You know, really unload everything on him and watch the church boy run for the hills. Oh Lord, I was so mean. So, I called him and he picked me up that night wearing his dress blues. He looked so handsome, and for a bit I almost lost my nerve. But when we got to dinner and he started asking deeper questions about me, I let him have it. I told him about the parties and the drinking and the abortion. I played it all off as a joke, as though this was exactly what everyone did in college. I expected him to get really uncomfortable. Maybe he'd end the date right there and call a cab to take me back to the dorm.

"But he didn't." She choked up, and it took a minute for her to regain her composure. "He just listened. And when I finished, he asked in the kindest voice I could imagine, 'Are you okay?' There wasn't any judgment or condemnation in his tone at all. Just genuine care and worry that I might be hurting. It was completely unexpected, and it broke me. I started weeping right there at the table, dead certain that was it. This guy was gonna run for it. But he surprised me again. He asked for a couple of to go boxes and paid the check. Then he took my hand, led me out to the car, and drove to the beach. It was mid-spring, and the days were just starting to get warm. We finished our meal on the hood of the car, and he told me about his life growing up. He told me about his abusive father and desperate mother. Of the grandma that took him to church on Sundays to get him out of the house. He told me how he'd found Jesus Christ, and how it had changed his whole life. Oh, the circumstances were the same, but his own fear and despair were gone. And he said that Jesus would do the same thing for me if I asked him to. He couldn't change the past, but I didn't have to carry it on my own anymore. He would save me from the guilt and the depression and the shame and all of it. It seemed way too easy, too cheap to be real. But I couldn't argue with what I saw sitting in front of me. Trevor was all sincerity, and nothing about him smacked of phoniness. I agreed to go to church with him that Sunday, and when the pastor gave an altar call, I went down to the front with Trevor and accepted Jesus as my Savior. All of the guilt and sadness I'd been carrying for months melted away at Christ's feet. He gave me a new life, even though I had nothing to give Him.

"So, you see, Jesus had already given me my life back, and he gave me even more in Trevor. He blessed me again when Amy was born. The abortion had damaged my uterus, and the doctors had told us it was unlikely that I would ever be able to get pregnant again. After years of trying, I was finally pregnant, and after a rocky pregnancy there she was. Our little girl, one I should never have been able to have. She was God's gift, just like Trevor. Just like my life. I had twenty years of joy with Trevor and almost 18 with Amy. Except for God's mercy, I wouldn't have had any of it.

"That's why I can't be mad at him now," she said. "Don't get me wrong, it hurts. It hurts just to breathe right now. But it's like Job said. The Lord gave. How could I fault him for calling my baby home?"

23

I didn't know what to say. I couldn't even figure out what to feel. Part of me wanted to cry, but another part still couldn't let go of the fact that God could have saved Amy, but didn't. Too many questions remained.

"Did Amy know any of that?" I asked.

Claire shook her head, sniffing. "Not for the longest time," she admitted. "I always thought I might tell her one day when she was older. It's one of the hardest decisions to make as a parent. How much do you tell your children about your life before Christ? How much do they need to know about your failings? I never lied to her. She knew that I lived a pretty immoral life before I met Trevor and got saved, but I never told her the details. She didn't know anything about the abortion. I think part of me was always afraid that if I was too free with what I told her, she might think that because I'd done those things and my life had still worked out that it would be okay for her to do them, too. Maybe it was silly, but that fear was always there.

"It wasn't until Saturday night that I realized she needed to know. After you left, I told her the whole story. Everything from my years of partying, to the abortion, to what Jesus did for me that Sunday... I think she was pretty shocked. It was hard to tell, as she was still a little drunk at that point, but she seemed really affected by it. She told me the next morning that she'd felt guilty because faith always seemed to come so easy for me and Trevor. Her questions and doubts made her think that she wasn't good enough to be saved. In all of our teaching her about Jesus and what he came to do, I guess it had all taken on a vague, ethereal feel. Jesus came to save people from their sins, yes, but we'd never really talked much about what that looked like in reality. She prayed the Sinner's Prayer when she was still a little girl, and Trevor and I both thought she was okay. She had questions as she grew, and we did our best to answer them. But whether she was ever really saved then or not, we failed to help her really understand that it was *her* sins, *her* shortcomings, *her* failings that Christ had come, not just to forgive her for, but to save her from! He could take all those doubts, along with the pain and tension she was feeling, and set her free from all of it!"

She disengaged the brake and wheeled her chair forward to the edge of my bed. Reengaging the brake, she reached out and took my hand.

"I hope you get to have kids one day. There's so much that God teaches you through them. About yourself. About himself. We definitely didn't do everything right, and I wish so badly that I could go back and be more intentional in teaching Amy about the Gospel. But I did get the chance to fix it.

"And she got it, Rudy. She was so excited to tell you. She was reading up for her paper on Oswald Chambers, when she came across a story about a time when he was really struggling with God."

I nodded. "Yeah, she told me about that on Friday. I guess he didn't think he was a very good person."

She smiled. "That's right. She read me one of his quotes from around that time. 'Either Christianity is a downright fraud, or I have not got hold of the right end of the stick.' I think he'd been saved years before, and he definitely knew more about God than most people in his day. But he struggled with his own sin. Until one day he finally let it go. He trusted God to do for him what he'd promised, and through that trust he found a love and peace in Christ that he'd never known before.

To my surprise, Claire actually laughed through her tears. "She was so thrilled. I was washing dishes when I heard her shout from the living room, 'Mom, this is it! This is it!' She'd tried for so long to earn God's approval. But she couldn't *do* anything to earn it. Just believe. It's all any of us can do at that point. But it's all God asks us to do.

"I went into the living room, and we prayed together. She asked God's forgiveness for everything and asked him to show her everything that Christ died to give her. 'I believe you, God,' she said. 'I'm so sorry for everything, but I need you. And I believe what you've said. I believe you'll save me.'

"She was so happy that night, Rudy. I wish you could have seen her. It was night and day from where she was Saturday night. God did answer her prayer in the end. He did save her. She died with faith and hope."

My eyes filled, and a tear rolled down my cheek. I was still angry, but I was glad Amy had finally found peace in all of this.

"Rudy?"

I looked at her.

"Do you have any other questions?"

I thought for a minute, then looked down and shook my head.

"Then let me ask you one. What are you really looking for, Rudy? Do you want answers *about* God? Or do you want God himself?"

I didn't answer. I couldn't.

"Can I pray with you?" she asked.

I shook my head. "Sorry, Claire. I appreciate you telling me all this, but I just don't think I'm ready for that right now. I still don't know that I'm ever going to be able to forgive him for letting her die."

She squeezed my hand. "Then know this. He's already forgiven you."

She went back to her room, but I wasn't alone for long. An orderly came in to move my bed down to the OR.

Everything Claire had said played over in my head. It was infuriating. My anger wanted free reign. God killed her. I needed to believe that. I needed to rage.

But I couldn't. Claire had taken the fire from my fury. And as they prepped me for the second of who knew how many surgeries on my leg, I felt calmer than I had in days. Not a good calm, though. My anger was gone, but all other feeling went with it. No joy, no hope, no rage. Just an infinite emptiness.

They wheeled me into the OR, placed a mask on my face, and I surrendered to the void.

They discharged me late the next afternoon. It was Sunday again. Barely a week since the last time I'd seen Amy, and already I was having a hard time remembering her voice.

The ride home was pretty rough. The cast on my right leg went from my foot to halfway up my thigh, so the only way I could sit in the car was stretched across the back seat. Getting in and out required acrobatics that would have been difficult even without a broken leg, but we managed.

First thing I noticed when Dad wheeled me through the front door was the smell of disinfectant. Judging by the strength of the odor, Mom must have unloaded an entire bottle of cleaner on the living room. Maybe two.

I felt bad, and made a mental note to apologize later.

Whoever designed my wheelchair clearly didn't expect to ever have to use one himself. To say the thing was uncomfortable would be a gross understatement, but for the next few weeks it would be the only way I could get myself around.

I wanted to be alone, but Mom and Dad had decided that was a bad idea. "You've spent enough time closed away in there," Mom had said. "You need to be around people now." They never made reference to the accident, the drinking, or any of it. I wondered how long it would take us to be able to talk about everything that had happened.

Within five minutes, I was bored. The light from the TV made my head hurt, an effect of the concussion that the doctor had described as "moderate-to-severe". It was like a weather forecast. *You've got a pain front moving in over your brain's left hemisphere. It's a doozy of a system and should bring with it moderate-to-severe pounding, along with sensitivity to light, sound, and generally any kind of consciousness.*

I almost laughed at the thought, but a fresh wave of dizziness prevented it.

So, movies and video games were both out of the question. Conversation was a no-go, too. With no other options left on the table, I asked Mom to bring a few books out from my room.

"Which ones?" she asked.

"Doesn't matter," I said. "Surprise me."

She smiled. Glad, I guess, that I was finally doing something that didn't involve pining for my dead girlfriend. A minute later she emerged from my room with an armful of books and set them on the end table next to me.

"Can I get you anything?" she asked. "Water?"

I shook my head. "Thanks, Mom. I'm good for now."

I turned to the stack that now represented my only possible source of distraction. It took a moment for my eyes to focus on the title of the first book.

The Life of John Wesley.

I chuckled in spite of myself. It seemed comical that after

all the time I'd spent trying to force my way through this book, now I wouldn't even need to. Thanksgiving was coming up in three days, and there were only three weeks left in the term after that. The decision had been made. I would focus on recovery now, and deal with finishing high school down the road.

But, with nothing better to do, I picked up the book and started flipping absent-mindedly through the pages. After more than two years in America, Wesley returned to England. I came upon this passage from Wesley's journal:

> *"It is now two years and almost four months since I left my native country, in order to teach the Georgian Indians the nature of Christianity. But what have I learnt myself meantime? Why, what I the least of all suspected. That I, who went to America to convert others, was never myself converted to God. I am not mad, though I thus speak, but I speak the words of truth and soberness…"*

I couldn't believe what I was reading. The leader of the Holy Club, the guy that thought himself so superior to everyone else that he jailed a doctor for breaking the Sabbath…he wasn't even saved!?

I read on:

> *"…But I speak the words of truth and soberness: if haply some of those who still dream may awake, and see that as I am, so are they. Are they read in philosophy? So was I. In ancient or modern tongues? So was I also. Are they versed in the science of divinity? So was I."*

He went on like that for a while, listing all of the things he had done. Giving alms to poor? Check. Well studied in the

Bible? Got it. Willing to suffer for the cause of the Kingdom? "I have labored more abundantly than them all," he wrote. But in the end, he concluded that none of it made him right with God:

> "Thus then have I learned, in the ends of the earth, that my whole heart is altogether corrupt and abominable, and consequently my whole life: that my own works, my own sufferings, my own righteousness, are so far from reconciling me to an offended God, so far from making any atonement for the least of those sins, which are more in number than the hairs of my head..."

I could empathize.

> "...that having the sentence of death in my heart, and nothing in or of myself to plead, I have no hope but that of being justified freely through the redemption that is in Jesus; that if I seek I shall find Christ, and be found in Him."

It was the exact same thing Claire had said. *She couldn't do anything to earn it. Just believe. It's all any of us can do at that point. But it's all God asks us to do.*

I closed the book and sighed. Something else Claire had mentioned had been nagging at me. *She prayed the Sinner's Prayer when she was a little girl... But?* I never thought there was supposed to be a "but." You prayed the prayer, and that was it. You'd declared your allegiance to God, and you were saved.

But saved from what? Guilt and lust and grief and all of it threatened to swallow me whole. And the inevitable question hit me.

Am I saved?

At first it seemed impossible. I'd prayed the prayer, gone to church for forever, believed in God and everything Christ had done. The works.

But the more I thought about it, the clearer it became. What are the Fruits of the Spirit? Love, joy, peace... Forget the rest, even just those three. Love? I'd told God I hated him more times in the past week than I could count. Joy? Haha, yeah, right.

Peace? Please.

Those things were supposed to mark the life of a Christian, but I didn't have any of them.

What are you really looking for, Rudy? Do you want answers about God? Or do you want God himself?

The thought came that God wouldn't want me. How could He after everything? The porn, how I'd treated my parents, the drinking, the wreck. Hating him. Now that everything was on the table, it was obvious that I'd never been saved. I'd been living as a hypocrite for years. And if there's one thing Christ had no time for in the Bible, it was hypocrites.

I tried to hold on to that. To make myself believe that I was beyond hope. But try as I might, too many voices shouted against me.

"It was her sins, her shortcomings, her failings that Christ had come, not just to forgive her for, but to save her from!"

"One day he finally let it go. He trusted God to do for him what He said He would do, and he found a love and peace in Christ that he'd never known before."

"I have no hope but that of being justified freely through the redemption that is in Jesus; that if I seek I shall find Christ, and be

found in him."

"While we were yet sinners…"

God wasn't the problem. I was. Chambers just had to let go. To trust God to do what he said he would do.

Amy did. Right at the end.

But could I? Too much still warred within me. How would I even know if anything was different? If I was saved? I'd thought I was for all these years, only to find out I was wrong. What proof would I have that things had changed?

I couldn't just let it all go. Maybe they could, great men like Oswald Chambers and John Wesley, and a woman as strong as Amy.

But I wasn't them.

24

I couldn't sleep that night. Being at home in my own room and my own bed was a far cry better than being confined to the hospital, but the pain and questions raged on.

And there was the computer. It was past midnight, and the house was dead quiet. Everyone else had gone to bed hours ago.

It sat there on my bedside table, taunting me. I kept trying to tell myself that I didn't really need to, that after everything I'd never need to again.

Images rolled in my head, things I'd watched on so many other nights, and a familiar curiosity made my blood run hot. Before I knew it, the computer had moved to my lap. The screen was on, and an Xpedition window was open.

Stealth Mode.

I hesitated. And something strange happened.

You don't need to do this.

My fingers hovered over the keyboard debating what to type.

I'll help you. They weren't lying. Just ask. I'll help you beat this.

It wasn't audible. I wasn't entirely convinced that it wasn't just me making up what I wanted to hear.

I'm here.

A tear escaped. Then another.

It didn't matter. It could be God's voice or it could be my own sleep-deprived mind. But I knew it was true either way.

God was there. So close I could almost touch him. And he was stronger than all of it. Just one question remained.

Did I want him to be?

I was so tired. Tired of fighting. Tired of grieving. Tired of asking question after question but coming no closer to the Truth.

So I gave up.

"Oh God," I cried, "forgive me. Please God, forgive me for all of it. Forgive my lust and my hate and the drinking. Forgive me for how I treated Dad. I can't do this on my own. I'm going to spend my whole life losing these fights. I'm so lost, God. I miss her so much, and I don't know how to move forward without her. But I have to, and I need you if I'm going to make it. Jesus, save me. Please, save me from this lust. Save me from this grief.

"Save me from me."

There was no voice from heaven. No electricity. No "Hallelujah" chorus.

But for the first time since I could remember, I didn't feel alone anymore. I closed the computer and tossed it on the beanbag chair, out of my reach for the evening. It was a gesture, as the last thing I wanted to do now was continue in Stealth Mode. The darkness had reigned long enough, and I wanted the Light.

I cried. For a long, long time, I cried. But it wasn't the despairing cry that had been my constant state for the past week.

No. The despair was gone. And something new was rising in its stead.

Hope.

Claire had been discharged a day before I was, and from what I heard she was staying with her sister. Like me, she was going to need help just getting around for a long time. It was good to know she wouldn't be alone.

Dad and I finally got around to talking. Monday morning, the day after God had finally gotten a hold of me, I joined him for breakfast and told him everything. I confessed about the porn and told him about when and how the questions had started. I apologized for what I'd said and how I'd acted. I told him about everything Claire had told me.

And I told him what God had done for me the previous night.

He didn't say much. Was dead quiet throughout my whole story, actually. But by the time I finished, there were tears in his eyes. He took my hand, and without a word to me started praying, thanking God for all of it.

I thought I knew him, but it's become ever clearer to me that I'm just scratching the surface of who Dad is. We've still got a long way to go, and there are a lot of wounds from the years that are going to take time to heal. But I think we're gonna get there.

Sim's a bigger question mark. He came over on Monday, and we talked for a long time. I told him pretty much the same thing I told Dad. It was awkward telling him about some of it, especially since I'd been a willing participant in SD cards and Stealth Modes. But he had to know. He had to know the answers I'd come to. Most of all, he had to know that God was real and just waiting for Sim to turn to him.

But when I was done, all he said was, "I'm glad for you, man. Boy, it's getting late..."

It was 4:00 p.m., but I could tell he was uncomfortable, and I let him go. I've been praying for him everyday, but the jury's still out on whether Sim will ever come to trust God.

Mark and Dani came over on Black Friday. We talked for hours about Amy and about Claire's thoughts on our questions. Dani had been digging deeper into the question of what the Christian life was supposed to look like and shared something she'd found in Galatians 5:16.

"'This I say then,'" she read in my living room. "'Walk in the Spirit, and ye shall not fulfill the lust of the flesh.' Then just a few verses down in 22 and 23 are the fruits of the Spirit."

Mark took over. "It looks like Paul is talking about his life in the flesh before Christ in Romans 7. That's when he couldn't do what he wanted to do and was a slave to the things he hated. But here in Galatians 5, he's laying out the difference between walking in the flesh and walking in the Spirit. It's night and day."

We all agreed to continue digging into that question, and by now it seemed like it might be the most important one we'd raised so far. The other questions affected our understanding of God, but this one cut to the very core of what our life in him would look like every day. Despite the lingering questions, we were all becoming pretty convinced that it was indeed possible to truly know both about God and to personally know him, too.

Amy's funeral was scheduled for Saturday, November 28th. Just two days after Thanksgiving. It was a strange time for a funeral, but life doesn't play by our calendar.

It ended up being oddly fitting. The entire affair was conducted as a giving of thanks for Amy's life, and everyone that spoke gave a testimony of how she had touched their lives.

I could see Claire's fingerprints on the whole thing.

She'd asked me if I wanted to say anything. The truth was, yes, I did. But I didn't trust myself to get out so much as an opening sentence before collapsing in a quivering puddle of goo. Dani stood in for me, and spoke about Amy with more emotion than I'd ever seen from her. I don't think there was a dry eye in the house by the time she finished.

I was grateful.

When we got home from the funeral, I retreated once again to my room. The door stayed open now. Just because Christ had saved me from the lust didn't mean I wanted to fight the temptation any more than I had to. If the door was open and people were home, then I was safe. At night now, the computer stayed in Mom and Dad's room. I'd never felt so free.

Despite not being able to bring myself to speak at her funeral, I felt like there was still so much unsaid. So much that needed to be said. I woke up my laptop and opened a new Word doc.

Amy,

Just got home from your funeral. I expected it'd be pretty bad, but it was all right as funerals go. There were a lot of people there. Mark and Dani came, and Sim, and a lot of your family. If you ever wondered whether or not your life touched the people around you, you should know that it did.

I miss you. Can't even tell you how much. If you can watch from up there, I guess you already know everything that's happened. I'm sorry. I know I probably let you down with all of that. I was an idiot, and it hurt so much having you gone. It's not an excuse, I know. But it is the reason.

You were right. I know you already know that. You'd probably say, "Well, duh!" and punch my shoulder. I wish you would. I'd give anything for you to make fun of me and hit me again.

But you were right. God got to me, and He showed me everything He showed you. I feel peace and hope for the first time in forever. It's like I've been living under a perpetual cloudy night, and I didn't think it would ever let the light through again.

I spent so long there. I guess you did, too. But I can see the sky again, blue and clear and beautiful, and I can feel the warmth of the sun on my face. It makes me cry when I think about it. I would have expected them to be tears of shame over the past, but they're not. It's all joy now, and hope for what's to come.

It does still make me sad when I think about that and realize that you won't be here to share it with me. I think about everything we were planning, and I wonder what it'll look like now with you gone. But I know that it will come, and I won't be as alone as I'd feared. God will be there. I always thought that was a cliché. But He really will. He's saved me from so much already, and I'm beginning to believe that maybe He's saved me for something, too.

I don't think I'll ever stop missing you, Amelia Davidson. And there's one more thing I need you to know. You saved my life. Your faith helped me to believe when things were at their darkest.

It makes me smile to think about what you're seeing now. I can't even imagine, but I know it has to be amazing. I'll be there soon to see it with you. Maybe you can show me around.

But God gave me back my life, and now I have to go live it.

I love you forever.

Rudy

ACKNOWLEDGMENTS

From the bottom of my heart, thank you for reading *Cult*. This story means a lot to me for a whole host of reasons, and I'm deeply honored to share it with you.

I owe my thanks to many other folks who helped shape *Cult* from its inception to the story you now hold in your hands.

To my first readers, Tarah Lewis and Stephanie Johnson, thank you so much for your time and generosity. And thanks for breaking the truth to me gently. You encouragement and insights were invaluable.

To my beta readers, Jennifer Johnson, Leilani Squires, Stephanie Flowers, Ryan Knight, Luisa Knight, Audrey Smith, and Tyler Pond (love you, bro), you all were fantastic, and your notes and encouragement helped to both refine the story and give me the drive to cross this finish line.

To my proofreader, Amy Eppley, thanks for your careful eye. Readers, any mistakes you happened to find are my fault. Amy caught them, I just missed removing them.

To Ben, thanks for your story notes. Without them, *Cult* would have been a very different and far lesser book. Can't wait to write with you in earnest.

To my parents, thank you so much for teaching me to love both reading and writing, and for instilling the reality of God and the truth of His Word in my heart from my earliest recollection.

And to my true First Reader, my beautiful wife, Tiffany, there aren't thanks enough to cover the countless late nights during which you watched the kids so I could get this book written, the countless discouraged moments you encouraged me through, and the unfailing support you've offered this story every step of the way. I love you forever.

How You Can Help Spread the Word!

Thank you so much for reading *Cult!* If you enjoyed this story, I'd appreciate it more than I can say if you could take the time to leave a review on *Cult*'s Amazon page. As a new author, reviews are a critical way new readers make a decision on whether to try a book like *Cult*.

Only about 1% of readers take the time to leave a review, which means writers like me treat every review, even the less-than-favorable ones, like solid gold. These reviews really do make a massive difference in our ability to grow our readership and continue to put out new work.

Thank you!

Stay Connected

If you liked this book, chances are you and I have at least a few things in common. I'd love to hear from you anytime at jl@jlpond.com. I also have a monthly(ish) newsletter where I share updates, sneak peeks, new book notifications, and more. If you'd like to be among the first to hear when something new is coming, you can sign up to receive that newsletter at jlpond.com/receive-newsletter.

I promise your information will never be sold, shared, or otherwise used in any purpose other than for me to touch base with you. And I promise to not flood your inbox with anything more than the occasional update.

www.ingramcontent.com/pod-product-compliance
Lightning Source LLC
Chambersburg PA
CBHW071308170626
46809CB00001B/367